FOX TROT

SHORT STORIES

For Margaret

FOX TROT

SHORT STORIES

Eugene McNamara

Black Moss Press

Published by Black Moss Press
2450 Byng Road
Windsor, Ontario
N8W 3E8.

Black Moss Press books are distributed
in Canada and the United States
by Firefly Books Ltd.
250 Sparks Avenue, Willowdale, Ontario, M2H 2S4.
All orders should be directed there.

Financial assistance towards publication of this book has been
gratefully received from The Canada Council, Department of Communications and
The Ontario Arts Council.

Layout and page design by Kristina Russelo
Cover art by Hervé Baudry

Canadian Cataloguing in Publicaton Data
McNamara, Eugene, 1930
    Foxtrot

ISBN 0-88753-255-1

I. Title.

PS8575.N34F69 1994   C813'.54   C94-900397-2
PR9199.3.M33F69   1994

ACKNOWLEDGEMENTS

Some of these stories have appeared in *Ontario Review, Canadian Fiction Magazine,
Antigonish Review, The Fiddlehead, Witness,* and *Prism international.* Several stories
were in the following anthologies: *Singularities* (Black Moss, 1990) *87: Best
Canadian Stories, 91: Best Canadian Stories.*

TABLE OF CONTENTS

But suddenly it was as though she had entered, and this appari-
tion tore him with such anguish that his hand rose impulsively to
his heart. What had happened was that the violin had risen to a
series of high notes, on which it prolonged without ceasing to
hold on to the notes, in the exaltation with which it already saw
the expected object approaching, and with a desperate effort to
continue until its arrival, to welcome it before itself expired, to
keep the moment open for a moment longer, with all its remain-
ing strength, that the stranger might enter in, as one holds a
door open that would otherwise automatically close.
         — Proust

FALLING IN PLACE

THE CHINESE GIRL AWOKE in the early morning still dark out and found her door unlocked. The corridor was empty silent under humming lights. The ward door was ajar. She remembered the story of the prisoner who found his cell door open and went out into the palace garden. There the poor wretch met a kindly reassuring priest who was in fact the Inquisitor. Soon the man was back in chains with the added torment of illusory freedom and false sympathy to goad him. The deepened horror.

But outside the hospital no false priest waited for her. There was only the parking lot lying there like a silent bowl of arc light. And she walked beyond it into the deeper inverted bowl of night. A deep pool starred with white water lilies. She had dreamed of rain. A school of small fish scattering in the deep. She saw them through circles on the blistered surface, thought of rain falling in a farmer's yard. Would his barn doors blow away in the wind? The hospital drains sang with rain.

Now she went up the grade to the tracks silvered in the fading moon. And she lay down across the tracks, cushioned her head on the chill steel and looked up into the slowly waking sky. Waited. *Oh my iron bridegroom* she said.

ON THE ROAD BESIDE the embankment the apprentice machinist drove in early light. He had wakened to a charley horse cursing limping in his silent morning house. Now he drove, the night mists wipered away, the radio in cadence. His mind was already in the plant. So many there were missing fingers. The machines were hungry. He feared them. At the morning break the men will speak of women. They want full bodied women. Somewhere else now women were breasting big waves on beaches the men will never see. The ditch beside the road was dry.

It had been a month of drought after a month of rain. He

7

had dreamed of rain. He thought of keeping a rain journal. How many days, how many inches, what damage to property, how some drown in cars in viaducts. Good for the crops some will say. But someone else will answer no, the crop's in peril. Not enough and the lawn burns. Too much and the picnic's ruined.

Never just right except in dreams where it falls like filmic mist in black and white movies of romance. Lovers dance in it.

Sudden there on the road in common light he heard the shudder of stopped steel on steel. Up ahead was the morning train shaking to a stop and someone *there*.

Oh God he thought and could only watch the meeting see it happen.

EVERYTHING WAS FALLING in place as the passengers fell forward. The train had leaned into its curve, righted on the straightaway and settled down. *Now* we thought. But instead we jolted from our seats in a hurtling protest of stopping. Then all was silent unmoving. We got off to see. There was blood on the sleepers. We turned to stare across the speechless fields at the still early sun. Tall weeds stood there helpless as any of us. Nothing could change now for her. The hard air stood still. It tasted like brass.

HE STOOD IN LINE at the supermarket docile thinking of nothing and then sudden as the wreck remembered it all. His hand on the brake. Futile. Nothing doing. Throwing up afterwards into his useless hands. And now here in the supermarket line ahead of him a row of grocery carts like train cars derailed, askew. Someone back in aisle four had dropped a jar of beets. A mess for someone else to clean up. And now someone's meat on the conveyor belt red as a kiss moved on added up put into a bag. It cannot be called back. The young woman ahead of him tells her child again that they cannot buy the cookies, that they have plenty at home. Does the child know it's a lie?

No, he thought. I am unfair. She soothes the child at home, reads him stories. Her kitchen is orderly and everybody keeps his or her voice down. Wildly, he looked back down the check-out line. He was square in the middle of it, too late to give up or move and more time to put in waiting. He thought I'd like to be a private detective, save people from blackmailers, sit back in a creaking chair, stare at the smoked window, listen to the secretary type reports, wait for the phone to ring. The girl's silver voice calls to him out of the dark wire, calling for help. He could save her.

A POET ONCE SAID that her eyes were the colour of sherry in the glass the guest has left. My eyes are like that. But here in the false dawn my eyes keep in them the deep shadows of night. Pillowed on the polished iron, I could see the morning glory clambering on chain link fences facing the embankment. Someone is hanging laundry on a line. White forms rising in the wind. I hear bird-song. A faint thrum in the rail. I lay down to sleep and I am certain to rise.

The weather conditions on that day: patchy morning fog thinning so that visibility was fair to good at the precise time of — And post incident analysis indicated no mechanical fault in the braking system. From the initial locking of the brakes to the point of impact —

The provenance of the engine: Electro-Motive Division, General Motors Company, London, Ontario, 1958.

There are several factors involved in braking: torque, brake shoe function, condition of track and gradient. The brake shoe bears against the revolving wheel with a radial force called *normal brake shoe pressure*. The retarding force of the brake shoe cannot be increased or prolonged indefinitely as train wheels may slide as a result of excessive braking force. (See H.J. Schrader, "Friction of Railway Brake Shoes at High Speed and High Pressure," *University of Illinois Engineering Experiment Station Bulletin* 301, 1938, Urbana, Illinois.)

There are other factors involved in acceleration and deceleration of course: speed, velocity (speed in a given direction) mass, air resistance or drag, acceleration and the rate of change in acceleration. Mass. The gross weight of the engine. The gross weight of the engine. *The weight of the engine.*

WHEN I finished hanging the laundry, I thought of cutting the roses back. They say to cut ruthlessly so they will grow more hardy. The cadence of my steps kept to the song we danced to last night. I was humming it and then I heard the chill cry and protest of the engine and then the day was nipped in the bud.

AFTER A LONG and aimless wait standing alongside the silent train, the passengers were put on busses. It was late morning. They were promised lunch in the next town. By now a kind of disaster-induced camaraderie had developed among them. A subdued cordiality ran through the busses.

I felt an odd lightheadedness, a feeling of post-excitement letdown. As the morning went on the things of our world slowly resumed their usual shapes. I smiled at my fellow voyagers. Everything seemed thick and alive and bright in the almost noon light. Just a little while ago it was all tenuous, fragile, brief and evanescent. I felt mildly hungry, on edge, jumpy, ready to burst into laughter or tears.

Then suddenly I thought of the first sight I had of the girl's foot next to the tracks as I stepped down from the car. Now all the air went just as suddenly out of the day.

ALREADY THE BLUE of the summer sky is turning harshly autumnal. The change has been both gradual and sudden. So also in a very brief time a man may be his actual age and simultaneously feel the swift errant emotions of childhood and youth. A man may feel grief over the loss of those periods of his life while at the same instant re-experience them. I did not know her name.

Thus I felt grief — not only for the wretched girl but for myself and my fellow passengers. Every previous experience of death came welling up. Pets, schoolmates, grandparents, friends, acquaintances, fellow workers. All crowded together in my memory in a hurly-burly of sorrow recaptured. The indifferent blue sky outside the bus window stretches on to everywhere anywhere and nowhere.

THE CHINESE GIRL had been studying music at the university. Her first piano recital (Erik Satie's *Gymnopedies* and *Nocturnes*) had been enthusiastically received by the faculty. The recital by one of her fellow pupils, a young man from a farm in the southern part of the Province, was attended with less warmth. This did not lessen the young man's ardor. He found the girl endlessly fascinating. Her eyes were like quick fish in deep water.

She was shy, elusive, reticent, dedicated and given to long hours of practice. There was not much time left over for romance. Still the young man persevered and a kind of wary relationship developed. She told him about her loneliness, her homesickness. He spoke with confidence of a two piano career for both of them.

Then came her time of retrospection, introversion, fear and collapse. She went into the hospital. The prognosis was positive. Her period of treatment would be brief, followed by outpatient therapy and a lighter academic load.

There had been a long dry spell of weather. The young man sat one afternoon in a coffee shop near campus. Some people came in and were talking to the waitress about the news. Gradually the story filtered through the damp air and the young man became aware. Rain fell that night like a breaking mirror.

THE APPRENTICE MACHINIST dreams of counter boring holes. This procedure would be followed by milling a flat space at the bottom end of the holes. He squinted through a fine spray of coolant. Metal chips lay like sharp confetti on the grim concrete floor. Tolerances were tight — plus or minus one thousandth. Next to him an old timer ran a big Bridgeport. On the other side was another old timer running an obsolete Milwaukee V Mill. Its age was covered with many coats of gray paint.

The apprentice's hands flew from the ball crank to the

reversing lever. His mind was busy with the examination he would soon take. Define running fit, push fit, force fit and shrink fit. Tables of stress conversion roll through his mind. His eyes are intent on the chips of metal curling and dropping to the floor.

And now without warning the accident flashes into his mind. Locked steel wheels grind and shear. In a grinding operation wheel and work must be kept in contact until sparks are no longer emitted. Define the function of a chucking grinder. Do not look into the shower of sparks. Do not look up into the morning sunlight. Do not look up at the tracks ahead of you.

THE RAIN FELL into the yard near the tracks. All the laundry is safely in, clean-smelling and folded. Lightning glints on the thorns of the cut-back rose bushes. The rain washes the tracks and sleepers, seeping into the roadbed gravel. Rivers flow into the lake.

THE RAIN FELL into the placid lake. The diesel horn mourned over the furrowed fields. Train going away someplace. Perhaps a bell on a wrecked ship far below is tolling. Caught in the currents off the Point, it might toll forever. Nobody there to listen. Bellsong sounds in ever-widening concentric circles.

I WENT BACK home. The apples were in. My father's orchard was full of pickers on ladders. Windfalls crushed underfoot. The air was thick and sweet. Bees hovered. We set up the old stand and sold jugs of cider to the tourists. I took my turns at the stand.

I tried not to think of her. But a glissando of notes fell in my mind, sharp as icicles breaking off a roof.

Su Lin at her recital. Thin, intent, as precise as the music. I saw her, not the tourists, not the bees slowly circling the cider jugs. Seeing her again was as tart as a bite into a green windfall.

The harvest is big this year. Truckload after truckload of tomatoes go past on the road to the canneries in Leamington. The subtle curve of the road at a point just past us causes the load to shift to the right. Then there is a four way stop. The load shifts again and the intersection is soon awash with tomato juice and loud with bee clamour. At night I dream of drowning with her. I hear a bell deep under water. The harvest is heavy this year.

I LAY DOWN on the sleepers so that I could rise again. I heard a final word spoken clearly. I told the doctor not to judge me. Nobody can know my pain. My fingers made music come from struck strings. Who could tell my fingers not to strike the chords? My love told me of his apple trees. He wanted to climb and pick the sweetest for me from the top. Oh my love, I cannot wait. I must lie down and wait to rise.

THE MORNING train comes and goes many times. Things become usual. Journeys are undertaken. The rain sweeps the train windows, certain as the last things.

Look Mommy, says a child as he points out the train window. *There's the sea.*

It's only a river, says the mother.

She does not look out the window. The train goes on, resolute, implacable as a final judgment. Its horn announces us. The river rises in the rain and flows on its certain way. We are almost home or going far from home. Everything is falling in place.

BROKEN CONNECTIONS

April 9, 1986

Institute for Spatial
Regeneration
Hacienda Del Mar
Credo, California

Dear Francis:

Incarnations and serendipity and hay presto and Im back in business again. This is truly a land of plenty. Its like a nineteenth century patent medicine ad. Theres a cure for just about anything.

I am in the guru business. I honcho a little encounter establishment and all the mighty of this earth are discovering me. Youd never guess how many cinema moguls, top brass in the recording industry, models, bright young men, politocos, international as they say jetsetters (whatever became of café society?) and other such like are so bloody insecure and unhappy that they fall all over themselves to give me money for the soul butter I lather them with. Imagine, giving money to a fake like me. You would never guess who I had (in all senses of the term) in the hot tub last night. She's that famous lady novelist Romona Clef. Not her real name but you get the picture.

Jessica is a key person on the staff here. Come to think of it, California was her true destiny. You should see her tan. You should see mine. I have this long guru beard and I look very spiritual. I suspect I am sounding in this letter like the phoney I am. The place is insidious. You begin innocently enough by saying something like hang in there or I know where you're coming from and before you know it, you're selling your soul to Count Dacron in a nauga-lined room for a dirty weekend with a teenager and you even call it a relationship. I may buy a fur lined van. See how far Ive sunk?

Why, you are thinking, is he writing me. Why? Because I need you out here with me. Francis, I need and crave your sober earnestness and good sense. We could be a team again. Joan has said no. She's teaching or something someplace my God in Ohio. Eheu. Ive had to enlist the services of this divorcée of a certain age keeping the books etc and also handling some of the meditation therapy sessions. If I keep up this pace my dick will fall off.

A man needs sanity somewhere in his life. Ive been lucky there. Up till now. Joan I mean. But now Im in munchkin land. I need your body. I need your soul.

You wouldnt have to sully yourself with the actual healing process if it bothered your conscience, which I suppose is still working overtime. You could confine your activity to the nuts and bolts of the place. Like Eichmann assigning boxcars as it were. But my little scam isnt all that bad. I may even be doing some good. Please dont think about it dear Francis. Just do it. Come on out.

    yr old companion
     Duffy.

P.S. Jessie says hello.

May 3, 1986
Toledo, Ohio

Dear Frank:

What a delight to receive your letter. Yes, I knew about Duffy's new venture and Jessica too. I suspect that he will really get some of those people out there so screwed up and dependent on him that he'll have to take them all to live in some jungle and get them all to drink poisoned Koolade.

I'm keepin very busy here, working for this educational tv station. I'm in charge of arts programming. Seems that they have an exaggerated respect for Canadian tv and my teaching experience takes on much weight with distance. They think I knew McLuhan.

Personal life isn't all that exciting. I read much of the night and do not go south in the winter. I went to a party given by one of the people in the department and it was so depressing I almost got sick. All clutching their drinks and swirling the ice cubes to simulate passion and sayin hi in bright voices. Am I crazy? There's a woman my age in the office who says things about her boyfriend. My god, am I a *girl?* Yes, sick-making. The idea of actually going on a date?

Duffy in California. My God. To work in a massage parlor all tarted up to be an Institute — I just couldn't hack that. I mean giving spiritual hand jobs to rich sickies.

Do you remember once asking me if Duffy actually did all those things he said he had? I mean helping with an exorcist? Come now, you might say. Well. I dont know. If you believe in angels, why not devils too? The thing is that Duffy is a story teller. That's all. He's always been one. Im not sure if even he knows whats true and whats a story. In a sense, he's still doing it, out there with the Terribly Anxious. Its a mistake to take him too seriously. After all, you have your own life to live.

Im happy to hear that things are très ok with you. Im coming your way in a few months and will probably prevail on you to take me some place nice for old times sake.

love, for old times sake,
   Joan

P.S. "Old Times Sake" is a phrase I seem to have picked up from Duffy's last letter. What old times?

May 7, 1986
Chicago, Ill.

Dear Joan:

Im happy to hear that you are getting your life in order. Ive been here about four months now. Im working on a magazine. It's a very specialized thing — for antique dealers. It is really a small operation and I have a lot of responsibility.

I just stopped and read the above. What a lot of blab. Im living on the near north side (I think. I can't get the borders of neighborhoods straight here.) near Graceland Cemetery. I walk past the place at least once a week. Ive been "dating" as you put it. Yes, it *is* embarrassing and awkward to be doing that at my age. Anyhow, she works as a receptionist for another office in the same building where *Antique and Arts Monthly's* (the plainness of the name is a clue to how square it is) office is. We met while we were waiting for the elevator. She's a widow with two children. They don't like me. I mean they suspect me of something.

Someone (I think it was you) once told me that there were only two ways to live. You can live on your emotions — I mean just follow them where they lead — into messy turmoil and to hell with the consequences. Or else you can try to live an ordered life. Sane. With borders on it. Chances are we all do both at different times. The romantic way leaves you open to a lot of hurt. So you retreat and try to put limits. Listen to Bach and make lists and show up for things on time. You wear a watch. You're responsible.

Am I making sense? There were times with you, or just thinking about you, when I thought—

Never mind. I think I'll send this without rereading it. Afraid if I did, I'd double think and probably hold back what Im trying so hard to stammer out. Try, won't you, to read between these shallow lines.

As ever,

Frank

June, 1986

TO: Francis ("Frank") Maxwell
FROM: L.T. ("Howlin Mad") Duffy
SUBJECT: Alternatives

OK So you dont want to go into the guru business. OK. I have these other ideas of ways we can as it were *make our mark*. Kick this one around a while: A loneliness machine. Which we can place in airport waiting rooms, train stations, bus stations, subways etc. You are lonely. You feel rejected. Nobody gives a damn. Wait. This machine does. You give it a coin and begin to tell it your troubles. The thing is that it listens. You have preselected the kind of voice you want to hear — I thought of a grandmothers voice saying over and over, *oh my poor dear* and *theyre just jealous* and *tsk tsk* — or a fathers voice saying *straighten up, be a man* — and maybe even a Mafia godfathers voice—

Well. You get the idea. We can iron out details later. Jessica (Jessie) Thomas thinks its a grand idea. We can offer you the Northern California district. Territory, I mean.

Wait a minute. There is also my other idea. A Garden For the Deaf. Or Theatre For the Deaf, with actors blowing up balloons with the speeches printed on them. Think of all the balloons inflating and deflating stichomithically (sp?) We could have different colors to signalize who has the leading role.

I think of the above that the Loneliness Machine has the most potential. Im a beehive of ideas. How about a First Stone Concession? Door to door. Be first on your block to cast The First Stone.

Seriously though, as afterdinner speakers used to say after the opening joke, things are going pretty well here. One of our clients is thinking of casting Jessica ("Jessie") in a movie hes making. No no no no, its not a casting couch thing. I suspect he fancies *me*. But if he did, and if she did, then Id be a little more short-handed here than ever and I need somebody I can trust.

Distance between us has made me appreciate you more, lad. I like the cut of yr jib. And as for the past—well, as I used to say, gaze not rearwards.

Here is a useful tract to conclude today's sermon: "Then Isaiah said unto Hezikiah, What said these *men*? And from whence came they unto *thee*? And he said *What have they seen in thine house*?"

World of comfort in those words. Think on them, lad, and think on my offer.

L.T. ("Howlin Mad") Duffy

June, 1986

Dear Frank:

I suppose you have this picture of me selling snake oil from the back of a wagon, eh? Far from it. Picture me instead in a white lab coat, grizzled, honest, quizzical expression on face, deep rabbi's voice, faint suggesting of Vienna connection around glottal stops—"Mister Ruban, we haf to get to the bottom—"

M. Ruban has certain problems in relationships. He thinks the problems have to do with a continuing inability to sever (these are his very words) his emotional dependence on his domineering mother, a matriarch named Iola who owns condos here and there and a whole block in Beverly Hills. Who needs severance.

All this Oedipus-shmedipus theorizing is his. I do not agree that the certain problems are due to Iola. Oh, she is a factor, yes. But it is more complicated than that alone. It's a slow process (sigh) and an expensive one (deeper sigh) but I have lots of time and he has lots of money.

M. Ruban is the noted producer of such treasures as *Golden Boys of the S.S.* and *Cheerleaders in Chains,* as well as some low budget motorcycle trash. (One of his relationship problems was this girl in *Cheerleaders.* To say more would be violation of ethics.)

M. Ruban is noted in the trade as a miracle man who does sound low budget work, which means that he can "bring it in for a million five, maybe less."

Im pairing him up, in a new therapy Im trying called "bundling" with a lady named Mignon who is very large in real estate (cunning, am I not? N.B. Iola's vast holdings) and who is currently suffering from these great fears, had gotten to point before seeing me where she wouldn't leave her home. Just sat there listening to recordings of storm troopers singing joyfully, Hitler's speeches. Like that.
Prognosis of both clients: guardedly hopeful.

But slow, slow and expensive.

So you see my dear friend, that this is not your ordinary cut-rate fly-by-night sleazy backroom abortion rip off pseudo quack phrenologist orgone box cultist operation. I am actually getting referrals from real doctors.

Eheu. The work proceeds. One sits here in the little office in the white lab coat, a clock ticking patiently and loudly, writing to the old confidant. One is fatigued, but satisfied—

yer friend,

Duffy

July 1986

Dear Francis:

So you are wondering about my career as an exorcist. You somehow have doubts about it. Why? Because I myself am, well. shall we say, a weak person? Do you doubt the existence of spirits? Do you doubt the existence of evil? Do you suspect that the Church doesn't dabble in such affairs?

Whichever, It does—I mean the Church—dabble, and It does— I mean evil existing—and I did. It wasn't *my* idea.

"No minister shall without the license of the Bishop of the Diocese, first obtained and had under his hand and seal, attempt upon any pretense whatever, either of obsession or possession, by casting and prayer, to cast out any devil or devils—-"

Look it up, if you wish, in *A Reporte of the Tormentes and Deliuerance of THOMAS DARLINGE, a Boye of Xiii yeares of Age That Was Possessed of SATAN.* Minister acted in good faith. Boy exhibited the usual: rolling and tossing, lying as though dead, convulsions, wild mouthings, often rude and offensive. Minister accused of cozenage, the boy cured.

Anyhow, I am out of that business. Wellllllllll, at least out of the Official Casting Out end of it. One might argue that the work I am doing here at the Institute is a kind of exorcising. One might. I do not.

Things go well here, even tho without your sound and steady presence. Joan tells me that you are still in the journalistic thing. Yes. We correspond.

There are people just like you all over the world. They, like you, take life with the seriousness they think it deserves. I, for my part, intend to go on as I am, treating life like the crude joke it is. Listen, Little Bilham. Live all you can etc.

I often ponder on you and the strange fate that took you to Chicago, the city of my youth where I havent been back to in yo these many years. Ah the place of my fair seedtime. If I looked back mebee Id turn into a pillar of something?

Ennyhow, as I picture you walking down streets I did also walk on, I get this funny (meaning odd, not ha-ha) stereopticon feeling. Everywhere Ive been is like an airport departure lounge.

Of course everybody Ive ever known does not exist. That's why Im writing to you, buddy. You alone arc possibly genuine, potentially authentik. Out here in Oz its all a sitcom that wont last the season.

There is always another season. There will always be devils to cast out.

Duffy

ps. Keep yr pecker up. Who knows? Maybe Ill be passing through Chicago sometime and we'll have a brew or two for olde tymes sake—

Sept. 1986

Dear Frank:

Your letter was finally forwarded to me and I'm sorry I didn't write to tell you that I was moving. The chance of a job with more responsibility and yes more headaches but more dollars was too alluring to turn down. Also, a chance to live in New York, perhaps the last chance in my lifetime, before they have to close it down, was too tempting. But how are you? How is your real life? I mean your dating and all—

I've been seeing a man. Or he's been seeing me. Whatever. He is nice and respectful and all but there's just no, well, spark? I think this thing with the man will run itself down and out in time. Soon, actually.

I've read your letter several times and tried to read between the lines as you said for what I thought was there. Maybe I read in what I wanted to be there—

Frank, my dear, sometimes I get lonely and frightened and I feel mortal and old—One of those times a week or so ago I almost called you up. It's at times like that when I'm grateful the Nice Man isn't around, because I think I'd marry him if he asked and it wouldn't be fair.

I think maybe you were going through something like that back when I first met you. Maybe you are building it up—building me up—in your mind now. Distance does funny things. But your letter did make me feel warm. I still hope to come through Chicago, but probably not until next summer. And I *will* call you when I do.

And maybe we'll see—

—As Ever,

Joan

Oct. 29, 1986

Dear Joan:

It was good to hear from you. I'm sorry/happy to hear that you're in NY: sorry for me, because you're further away from me, and happy for you because it's what you want, I guess. Things here are settling into a kind of routine, as I guess life anywhere does. It's both comforting and boring.

The job is slow, but so is the antique business right now. I think I could put the magazine out all by myself, working just fifteen minutes a day. But of course Parkinson's Law (is that who it is?) applies and the staff manages to keep on looking busy.

The lady I was seeing. Well, we decided, mutually, that it wasn't going anywhere. I suppose her children are relieved.

A funny thing happened on my lunch hour yesterday. I went for a walk in Grant Park and got myself involved in a game of touch football with a bunch of guys from other offices. I hadn't touched a football since I was in the novitiate.

The sound of a kicked football always means autumn to me. An exciting sound. But it's also the hour before the evening meal and the grand silence, and those high ceilings in the corridor leading to the chapel. All along the corridor, pictures of past Superiors are hung. Those funny nineteenth century photos where the eyes are so clear. I suppose playing football was to keep us from concupiscence. Back then, everything had a reason. But yesterday was just for fun.

Duffy keeps writing to me. I don't know if he's serious about wanting me out there in his Disneyland or not. Probably it's Just Duffy talking. Anyhow. About you. How are you?

Write, please, when you get time—

love, Frank

Oct. ?, 1986

Dear Frank—

.I dont know how to begin this—But I thought you might wish to know anyway—Duffy died—it was very sudden—In the midst of a therapy session—The client got very agitated and hysterical—so things were very hectic for awhile—

Im sorry to have to bother you with this sad news, but I didn't know who else to turn to—Mr. Ruban has been very very kind and helpful—He plans another movie soon and this time my part will be bigger and won't be cut out—

But the Institute is in really bad trouble—financial—and there is a limit to what I can ask of Mr. Ruban—Duffy took out several loans I didn't know anything about—I am not liable, but the bank is looking for somebody to hang it all on—I don't know why he borrowed money as there was a lot coming in from the clients—

Frank, there are no relatives—no family, except us— I had him cremated and sent the ashes to you.

I think perhaps you are the best person to decide how to dispose of him—I don't know where Joan is —

Duffy often spoke fondly of you—especially during this last difficult period—I think he regarded you as a son or younger brother—

I too often think of you—I think you came to the office when I was going through a bad unsettled time in my own growth to personhood—and so I wasn't able then to respond to what I thought you were saying so silently—
Still I hope to see you again—perhaps you'll come out this way?

As Ever,
Jessie

Letter received by F. Maxwell. Postmark California. No salutation.

October, 1986

In the night sky in October, Venus is practically unseen, and sets less than an hour after the sun. Mercury is a morning star, as is Mars, while Saturn and Jupiter are evening stars. Jupiter, however, is too near the sun to be seen. Saturn, on the other hand, is easily seen all through the night, moving slowly westward, brighter than anything else in its sector of the sky. Uranus cannot be seen until later in the month and Neptune is drowned in the sun's setting.

Neptune is drowned in the sun's setting.
Neptune is drowned in the sun's setting.
Neptune is drowned.
Drowned.
(unintelligible line)

Letter returned to F. Maxwell.

A small hand, index finger pointing has been stamped next to F. Maxwell's return address in the upper left corner of the envelope. Returned is printed across the top of the hand. The last letter (d) of the word is just at the cuff of a shirt which covers the wrist at the end of the hand. The beginning of a coat sleeve is just behind the cuff. The words *undeliverable as addressed* are printed below the hand.

(RETOUR) RETURN TO WRITER is stamped above and to the right of the pointing hand. INCONNU (UNKNOWN) is stamped to the right of Joan Duffy's address. The address F. Maxwell thought was hers. All of this is stamped in faded red ink.

Sept. 20, 1986

Dear Mr. Maxwell.

I am a graduate student at Tecumseh and am working on the works of L.T. Duffy (1920—) for my thesis. I understand that you were close to him during the time I am tentatively calling "The Long Silence." There are, you see, persistent rumors that during this period when he did not publish anything he was at work on a long poem. Other critics theorize that this poem is really the work of Joan Duffy, his estranged wife, I do not know if you can shed any light on this matter. I understand that you know her also.

Another problem is my exegesis of "The Triumph of David," A Duffy poem originally published in *Canpo* and then collected in *Things That Break*. It is my position that this poem has not received sufficient recognition, even though two articles have appeared on it (one in *Tecumseh Review* and the other in *Slow Artichoke*.)

In view of your association with Mr. Duffy, I wonder if you could be of assistance to me and take a few moments to answer the following queries:

1.   To your knowledge is this poem allegorical?
2.   What is the significance of the musical procession?
3.   If whole poem allegorical, are cherubs part of it?
4.   Why decapitated giant's head?
5.   Pastoral archway and tree. Are these escape to reality ala *Ordinary Time,* poems?
6.   "Innocents," Line twenty. Does Duffy posit salvation through child-like innocence? As in "Night Watch?"

I hope a few moments consideration of the above will not impinge on your time.

Thanking you in advance,

Sincerely,
Gunnar Welt.

P.S. I wonder if you have a current address for Mr. Duffy. I understand that he is living in California someplace. Also Ms. Joan Duffy?

An excerpt from Patrick & Mitchie, Booksellers Catalogue 68: Modern Poetry (p.3)

Dickey, James (1923—) *The Shark at the Window*. Broadside. Palaemon Press. n.d. 1 of 26 copies lettered and signed by the poet. fine.$50.00

Dennis, Albert (1915-60) *Wednesday Morning*. 8 vo cloth
N.Y. (1940) fine, lightly rubbed d.j. $25.00

Duffy, L.T. (1920-86) *Ordinary Time*. Samson House. Toronto. (1966)
a copy for review with slip from the publisher $20.00

Things That Break. Samson House, Toronto. (1978) Second printing of the trade edition fine in d. j. $20.00

Dobrich, Boris. (1922—   ) *Sorrow at Fort Zinderneuf*. Harner. N.Y.
(1966) fine. $50.00

Excerpt from press kit for *Sudden Deadly*, a Zenith Corporation release. Ruban Productions Inc.

Jessica Webb was born in Birmingham, Michigan to parents originally from Ontario. Her mother was a ballet dancer and her father a high school teacher. Early dance training lent grace to Jessica's fresh-scrubbed beauty—qualities which led to local modelling contracts at age 14. Within a year she was on the cover of *Teenie*. She switched to an acting career the following year. After appearing in a summer stock production of *Our Town* she auditioned for the television series "Fame" and for Joseph Papp's New York Shakespeare Festival. After a brief detour as Personal Assistant to the late poet-guru Liam Duffy she caught the keen eye of "Benny" Ruban who cast her as the kooky girl in his celebrated update of *Amboy Dukes*. Her role in *Sudden Deadly* as the young girl—young enough to be Marlow's daughter and old enough to seduce him—is the fullest showcase of her talents to date.

Item from *Northwestern Alumni Times*.

Nuptial News: William Pierce ("Bud") Webley (BUS '60) and Joan Evans Duffy (GRAD '67). After a honeymoon in Italy and Greece, the couple plan to reside in Manhattan where she is Professor of English at Marymount College. Mr. Webly is President of Compusystems in Flushing, N.Y.

Frank took the shoebox off the table and went out. It was about eight o'clock and already dark out. He shifted the box under his arm and turned the collar of his jacket up. It occurred to him that wearing this pea coat made him look like a sailor on shore leave, out for a good time.

He walked up to Irving Park and turned left. The low fence was just ahead. The wall on Berteau Street was lower than the gate but it was topped with barbed wire. Berteau Street was as dark and silent as the cemetery. Halfway down, neon light from a bar cut across his path. Music came from inside. Country western.

Past the bar, up near the corner, he stopped, looked back down the street and then hunched himself up the wall. He pushed the shoebox under the barbed wire and turned it over so the ashes could spill out.

Then he dropped back to the sidewalk, placed the shoe box at the curb's edge and went back down the street. The song on the jukebox as he came in was about cheatin and slippin around. There were only three customers in the place. Two old men were at a table. A large woman was at the bar drinking something that looked tropical and out of season.

"Draft beer," said Frank. "Make it two."

"Got an invisible friend?" the woman smiled.

"No," said Frank. "Not invisible. He's dead."

"Oh," she said. "Listen, I am sorry—"

"It's ok," said Frank. "He wouldn't mind a little joke. I'm sort of having these in his honor."

He tilted one of the glasses in a ceremonial way towards the woman and took a sip. She smiled uncertainly and half raised her own glass. Then Frank made the same gesture with the other glass towards the door.

"Peace," he said.

"Is this the night we change the clocks?" the bartender said.

"I don't know," the woman said. "You spring forward and fall back, right?"

"I was in love with his wife," said Frank. "But he ran off with my girlfriend."

"That is tough," said the woman. "Industrial tough."

"They went to California," said Frank. "But he's buried back here."

"Don't forget to change your clocks," the bartender called after Frank as he went out.

"Keep in touch," the woman called.

"I won't," Frank said. But the door was already closed behind him.

He had the feeling of something undone. A letter to write to someone, a bill to pay, a connection to make. He could not think of what it might be. He walked down the dark street towards the lights.

SCENES FROM THE CIRCUMNAVIGATION OF THE GREAT WHITE FLEET (1907-1909)

That's not what it really was called. "Great White Fleet" was some journalist flight of verbal fancy. It was the Grand Fleet or the Battle Fleet or most properly the Atlantic Fleet. Yes, the ships were white. The U.S. Navy was singular in the world in persisting to paint its warships white. After the dingy grey Japanese ships kicked the bottom out of the Tsar's gaily painted fleet most of the world's sea powers went grey. Not the U.S.

Teddy Roosevelt couldn't keep his hands off his Navy. He thought it would be a splendid idea to send his Atlantic fleet into the Pacific and then around the world. His canal in Panana wasn't quite finished, so the first leg of the trip would be down the coast of South America, through the Straits of Magellan, past such ominous sounding points of reference as Point Famine and Desolation Island, where they would be hit by immense tides, the fierce williwaw wind, maelstroms, and water spouts. And all along they would be plagued by spies, anarchists and the everpresent freemason plot.

It wasn't a brand new idea. There were lots of naval courtesy calls from one country to another. It was all part of the bullying, gesturing, posturing, bluffing and jockeying for power that went on early in the century. Admiral Mahan said that to be a Great Power you had to have colonies and then a big navy to protect them. Small countries went bankrupt just to buy one or two battlewagons. The public loved battleships. Prints of the big ships foaming at the bow and emitting clouds of smoke were hung in schoolrooms. England had more battleships than any other country in 1907. Sherlock Holmes was always worried about secret plots to steal British navy secrets.

Navy officers hated those courtesy calls. Civilians gawked all over the ship, the guns were hung with bunting, speeches were declared from the top of the forward turret, the band played and they had to dance with guests under the guns. There are photographs of sailors dancing with one another on Admiral Dewey's flagship just before the battle of Manila Bay. The Admiral did not object. Yes, there was some faggotry in the Navy. Many sailors were homos. Some were brawling thugs, drunkards, yeggs on the lam.

Now, T.R. decreed, we need a better class of bluejacket. How could you garner any prestige from shore leave parties of fairies and thugs? A vigorous recruiting drive was launched using a brand new slogan: *Join the Navy and See the World.* Lots of rosy-cheeked teetotaling farm boys from the midwest signed up.

Most courtesy calls had been fairly local. The big ships burned lots of coal and required constant mechanical tinkering. The ship's innards were crowded with brass gauges, slapping pistons, clanking chain shafts, ammunition hoists, turret-turning engines—all demanding nearby repair shops. Coaling stations had to be available.

None of this daunted T.R. He had been sending his navy here and there, showing the flag, interfering with all sorts of European power maneuvers. The Europeans feared that this impulsive American President would precipitate a war with Japan. So did Canadian Prime Minister Wilfred Laurier who predicted giant sea battles off the coast of British Columbia. The Hearst newspapers were full of Yellow Peril talk. There were race riots in California. T.R. talked softly, hid his big stick under the desk and went on with plans for the voyage.

Some of the officers went to hear Caruso in *Rigoletto* just before the fleet sailed. The young officers were a handsome lot. They had just won the Army-Navy game. They were stout-hearted fellows. At a banquet they shouted huzzahs for Admiral Evans. They did not know that he suffered from gout. Second to Evans was Admiral Thomas who was overweight and had a weak heart. Third in line was Admiral Sperry who was in ok health but suffered from an uncontrollable tic in one eyelid that made it appear as if he were winking in a flirtatious or conspiratorial manner. The last of the Admirals to go on the trip was Big

Bill Emory who had no health problems. But he insisted on taking his dog, little Bill, along on the voyage. Little Bill would embarrass the fleet in many ports. He was flatulent. Little Bill, not his master.

All of these flag officers were long in the tooth. But worse, none was a diplomat. They faced fourteen months of smiling, dancing, incessant drinking of toasts, eating too much and listening to—and making—speeches.

The ships were in shabby condition under the new coats of white paint. A lot of slipshod engineering and pinch-penny funding had resulted in cracked boiler tubes, poorly designed hoists in open shafts with no safeguards against sparks from the gun breeches wafting down to the powder storage. There were cracks in the armor plating. There were rumors of graft and pay-offs to government inspectors.

Some of the ships were obviously over the hill. The *Kearsage* had only puny eight inch guns and was covered over with wood painted to look like armor. The *Maine* (not the one which was sunk in Havana—this was the second ship to bear the name) burned an enormous amount of coal. A collier had to be lashed alongside and fuel parties passed bags of coal across to be hurled into the ever-hungry furnaces. The newspapers said the fleet was awesome, formidable, invincible and intrepid. In fact they were sixteen wallowing energy-wasting examples of maritime obsolescence. The British *Dreadnought* was launched just as they sailed. Her complement of twelve inch guns made her a match for any two or three of these white seagoing elephants.

A fifty mile an hour gale hit and the farewell dance on the *Connecticut* was cancelled. The Japanese stewards had been fired from the battlewagons. They were replaced by Negroes who had joined up to see the world. These men became disgruntled darkies, sullen and uppity because all they got to see were the galleys.

The storm broke. Ten crates of Bibles were taken on board. The bands played "The Girl I left Behind Me." The bulldogs of the sea weighed anchor. A flotilla of small boats followed them out. One was filled with officer's wives weeping and waving handkerchiefs. Another was full of spies, all taking notes, peering through brass telescopes, making secret freemason signs to one another. They were so busy making notes and signs and peering that they almost collided with the Harvard rowing team. The Yale and Harvard rowing crews bent to the oars and raced under the bow of the *Illinois*. Little Bill barked down at them. A young man named Porter in the Yale scull was inspired to write a song which later became his school's football fight song.

This was the New Navy. Showerbaths had been installed. There were pianos to gather around when off duty. There were barbershops and nickelodeons. Toothpicks were issued and men were drilled in their use. The new swabbies bought red jaw-breakers and licorice whips at the canteen. There were print shops aboard and each ship had its own daily newspaper. Each ship had its own amateur theatre company and rehearsals of minstrel shows added more to the rancor of the black stewards. Each ship had its own library with books on travel and etiquette. Stockrooms were filled with boxes of bonbons to be given to foreign ladies. Dancing lessons were conducted on the foredeck. Midshipmen kept watch so that nobody could cut in. Daily inspections were held to be sure that nobody got tattooed.

But nothing could stop the insidious spread of the freemason conspiracy. A copy of *Morals and Dogma of the Ancient and Accepted Scottish Rites of Freemasonry* (1871) was discovered in an ensign's locker. Wands, badges, swords, aprons and ceremonial books were found secreted on the ships. This was a time of constant fear of sabotage. Anarchists and unfriendly foreigners were always attempting sabotage. Coal taken on board was carefully checked. In Trinidad some sticks of dynamite were discovered in a coal pile on the dock. One suspected stick of dynamite was found to be a wand used in freemason rituals.

Conditions below deck were frightful. In the furnace rooms men collapsed in the hellish heat. In the first two months of the voyage, twenty-two coal passers went insane. Each ship had its own alienist. Some of these doctors were given over to the practice of a new theory of mental illness. These physicians spoke in Viennese accents and insisted that the sickbays be provided with leather couches. Soot-begrimed sailors were forced to recount their dreams and secret fantasies.

Above deck, men were being groomed for shore duty. They had to appear ruddy and innocent. That left out the Negro stewards and the black gangs, pale under the coal dust. The men chosen looked innocent enough, but the brass still feared gaffes and incidents. They invented a kind of shore leave police which would be called The Shore Patrol. They would follow the men about to be sure that they did not smoke, drink or consort with the inevitable women of the ports.

The shore leave parties took lessons in charm, urbanity and culture. They studied languages. Soon all could speak French and German. Spanish and Japanese were frowned on. But some learned those languages secretly. Some secretly learned Danish.

In their free time the boys played Indian, played Peck's Bad Boy type pranks on the officers, ate ice cream, danced cheek to cheek, played football on deck, tap danced on the forward guns and behaved like jolly tars. The coal threw a lot of soot on the ship's white paint. In between football games and bags of water dropped on officers the men had to form painting parties to keep the ships looking pristine and bully.

Off the coast of Rio de Janeiro a ghostly wooden ship steered into the fleet formation, nearly colliding with the *Louisiana*, Ominous portent. But the Brazilian welcome soon made them forget the strange apparition. Small boats full of darkeyed women blowing kisses and men waving straw hats bobbed in the harbor. The anchor chains went down and the guns went up. Days of breakfast speeches, endless presentations of loving cups, compulsory attendance at Mass, cable car rides up the mountian to luncheons, garden parties, teas in the botanical garden, and evening banquets began. The fleet gave a reciprocal dance on the *Connecticut.* Women in velvet dresses, ruffled blouses and picture hats were whirled about the foredeck, taken on tours below deck, groped and kissed in dark corners. Some of these women filched the ship's silverware, tucking a fork or spoon into a fur muff.

But there were more than a few tears in the sailor's eyes when the visit was over. Some men had fallen in love and leaped overboard. Others accidentally fell in. A piston on the *Maine* cracked. She sputtered and limped. Her coal consumption doubled. The coal passing parties sped up their work. Bags of coal were hurled across. Some were missed and burst against the superstructure. Soon the decks were awash with coal. A perpetual painting party worked on the *Maine's* hull.

A midshipman on the *Kearsage* threatened to reveal Masonic secrets. He was clubbed into insensibility and thrown overboard. It could have been worse for him. The oath he had taken spoke of throat cutting or having his tongue torn out if he violated the oath.

They had forty-six thousand miles to go. In Japan a government decree was issued in advance of the fleet's arrival. Sticks and stones were forbidden to be thrown at dogs accompanying the sailors. The sailors should not be stared at except if and when "necessary." Sailors on bicycles should not be pelted with stone, tile or dung. Americans were reputed to be disgusted by the sight of people spitting in the street or littering. Such practices were forbidden during the visit. Nobody should ask the ages of the sailors unless "necessary."

Obviously nothing was being left to chance. Paper lanterns were hung. Kimonoed girls practiced simpering and enunciated *I love you very much.* Teapots simmered. But the government was uneasy. Who knew what the madman T.R. really planned? And the ultranationalist Black Dragon Society was rumored to be in league with the international anarchists and freemasons.

The officers kept a watchful eye on the enlisted men. The Japanese had barrels of beer and geishas—hundreds of each—ready for the shore leave. The officers insisted on ice cream—vanilla—and no ladies. One man off the *Kentucky* was driven to drinking lemon extract. He went mad, was psychoanalyzed, but died anyway. He was permitted a secret military funeral. When his body was prepared for burial a freemason's ceremonial apron was found under his uniform.

The officers had their own troubles. Their Japanese hosts kept pressing the booze at them. The officers tried to couple diplomatic graciousness with limitation. The Japanese officers at a banquet grew more and more hilarious as the evening wore on. They ended by throwing Admiral Sperry onto a blanket and tossing him in the air three times. The alarmed Americans later learned that this practice was considered a great honor to the tossed person. The American officers tossed Admiral Tojo in the air. Blanket tossing, as well as elocution and tap dancing, was added to the program of instruction at Annapolis after this voyage.

The Japanese bands played "Dixie," "Yankee Doodle" and "John Brown's Body" as the fleet left the harbor. A chorus of *I love you very much* and *sayonara* crossed the increasing gap between the shore and the ships. The men, bloated with tea and ice cream, belched in response.

Admiral Evan's gout kept him confined to his room. Admiral Thomas died enroute to China and was buried at sea in his full dress uniform. It was whispered in the focsle that the full regalia of a Grand Master lay under his gold epaulettes. Admiral Sperry conducted the service, winking incessantly. Little Bill barked, bit a bosun's leg and peed on the deck as the body was consigned to the deep.

In China, the Dowager Empress waited for the big white boats with fear and anxiety: Her palace was a honeycomb of plots and counterplots. Even here, in the Forbidden City, the freemasons had penetrated. Natural disasters—flood and famine—along with rival opium cartels, revolutionaries, pirates, smugglers and squabbling warlords combined to give her a migraine.

Then the fleet kept hemming and hawing about just which Chinese port it would visit. One was too shallow, another too close to Japan's waters and that would offend them, another had this or that lacking. The Welcoming Committee scurried north and south and finally in a rather desolate place called Amoy they erected a Pleasure City. It was like a siege fortress. Once the shore leave parties were inside, the gates were locked. A big fireworks display set fire to the pavilions. Escaping sailors looted the ruins before they left.

In Australia some enlisted men tried to pay for souvenirs with Confederate money. They looked at a papier-mâché *Mayflower* with jaded eyes. Officer's wives who had followed the fleet on the liner *Bremen* were featured in the Sydney rotogravure sections. Hospitals were full of people trampled in crowds. A bridge collapsed under the weight of sightseers. Rampaging trolleycars ran pedestrians down. Two hundred and twenty-one sailors fell in love and successfully jumped ship. Decades later these deserters were the cream of Australian high society.

By now none of the ship's company could stop smiling. Even when they were not in port the officers barked stern orders through a grin. The men obeyed in a sluggish and sullen manner but with happy, goofy smiles on their faces. The fleet donated food stores to earthquake victims at Messina. This included the last of the bonbons. The White Star liner *Republic*, coming with a load of new supplies, was sunk in a collision with the *Florida*. Meat was purchased from a slaughterhouse in Marseilles.

By the time the fleet reached Gibraltar the meat was found to be contaminated. The sailors cursed in French. Soon the waters off the big rock were filled with dumped carcasses. Reports from North Africa held that the stench from the rotting meat was persistent for over a week. British, French and Russian battleships were anchored off Gibraltar. As the U.S. fleet came near, bands struck up and four national anthems mingled in a cacophony of nationalism. It made dancing on the foredeck impossible.

Back home, teddy bear sales were way up in toy stores. Pictures and models of battleships were hot items too. Boater hats for women became a rage. This was not a time for shirking or sinking into a blue funk. Yessiree the bluejackets were on their way home.

Meanwhile the ships slumped on the last leg of the journey. Pistons slammed, valves leaked steam and hot water, soot smeared the hulls. The store of white paint was running out. The dress uniforms were a bit ragged and turning a stubborn washed-out grey.

The men were too tired to dance or get haircuts. They didn't even play Indian. The food—hardtack and bully beef borrowed from the garrison at Gibraltar—did not require cooking so the Negro stewards finally got to come up on deck and see at least some of the world. The *Kearsage* and *Maine* were far behind, straining to see who would be last in line. Nonetheless it had been all a splendid effort, an exercise in pugnacious pageantry.

Little Bill had not survived to bark and fart at the welcoming boats. Someone—an anarchist or freemason or uppity Negro or perhaps merely anybody sick to death of the animal's ceaseless barking—had hurled him overboard. Crowds of wives, sweethearts, whores, sluts and transvestites in fur-trimmed coats waved from the dock. Boatloads of spies kept pace with the lead ship. Admiral Sperry smiled and winked at a transvestite in a Directoire gown and picture hat. Below decks, insane men in chains raved. Negroes sulked. Tattoo artists waited on shore.

The fleet had been out for four hundred and thirty-four days, had touched the equator six times, been to twenty-six countries, carried fourteen thousand men, consumed four hundred and thirty-five tons of coal and exploded, in ceremonial salutes, one hundred thousand pounds of powder. No record was kept of how much ice cream had been ingested.

While Admiral Tojo had been waiting for his turn to be tossed on the blanket he noticed the severe face of a young American ensign. There was something different about that face, something not quite like the boyish, open, innocent—or ignorant—look he had seen on the other young officer's faces. He asked an aide, sotto voice, to find out who the officer was. Then it was his turn on the blanket.

The next day Tojo received a report from a spy.

"The ensign's name is Halsey. His superiors say that he shaves with a blowtorch."

"A blowtorch?" the Admiral frowned.

"His code name is *Bull*," the spy went on.

The Admiral stared thoughtfully out the window.

"All Americans are crazy," he said finally. "A blowtorch."

After T.R. welcomed his big fleet home, he left office. Now he felt free to travel abroad. He went to Europe and went horseback riding with the Kaiser. It was splendid. He went to Queen Victoria's funeral. He went hunting in Africa and killed two hundred and ninety-six animals. He liked to do that. It was bully.

TRAVELLING WITH STRANGERS

I went down on one of those really hot days when nobody even says hot enough for you and people walk slowly in dazzling light. It was a good time for drinking beer in a dark place. So I found one and sat at the bar which was horseshoe shaped. What faced me across the bar was a man in his sixties with a completely bald head. A young woman, maybe in her late twenties, sat very close to him.

"How's the new car?" the bartender said.

The bartender had one foot up on a case of empties and leaned a hip against the sink.

"You know the first thing I did, day it was delivered?"

The bald man's voice was deep, growly, resonant as if coming from a tunnel. The voice seemed to originate somewhere in his feet.

"First thing I did was drain all the oil out of the sucker and replace it."

"Uh huh," the bartender encouraged.

"And you know what kind of oil I put in?"

"No," said the bartender.

"Quaker State," the voice went on with a tone of triumph. "Best fucking oil—the *only* oil—"

Then there was silence, except for the tv which was on and nobody was looking at it. Some exotic sport. Kickboxing maybe. I wondered what kind of oil was in my car.

My daughter has joined one of those cult religions. They live in migrant worker style shabbiness. They grow and harvest cabbages and sell them at the airport. I picture businessmen hurrying toward departure gates and wondering how to fit a cabbage into an attaché case. My daughter previous to this excursion studied dance, photography and piano. At different times. I remember her final piano recital.

On the hot day when I sat in the bar feeling judged and

found wanting by the bald man who swore by Quaker State I was on my way to visit my brother who lived in—I do not know what to call it. Our society has trouble with these matters. We distinguish between *nursing* homes and *rest* homes and speak of *placement* and institutions are called *facilities*.

I love Ravel's music for solo piano. It has an innocent quality, paradoxically mingled with slightly jaded regret.

I wanted to tell my brother about the strange urge I have to call our father on the phone. He has been dead for forty years. The last time we spoke I was a young snot. Now I would like to let him know that I have not been a complete flop in life.

How are you, son? he might say. And I'd say *Just fine*. Then there would be uneasy silence, like the wariness between two animals met by chance.

I want to tell him everything I've done and how well my children have made out. Except for my daughter who labours in the fields for a charlatan who drives around in an air-conditioned Rolls Royce. I want to tell my father about these silly bouts of self-consciousness and fear of failure that continue to haunt me. How I dread the mornings, how I edge warily into the day. About the women who were married to me or who loved me or rejected me. I still smart about my overboard folly and tempestuous hurtling after a young woman (this was back in my thirties—late and dangerous thirties) who did not give me a thought.

Is that so, son? my father's voice will come over the wire. But that would be all. There would be no final healing word, no wisdom proffered. My brother would not understand this desire to call our father. My brother lay in a blissful fog of unknowing.

Not long ago I was talking to someone I hardly knew and after a little while I found myself *explaining* and justifying my life. Who are these people and why do I allow them to judge me?

My second wife liked to read those bodice-ripping romances. She devoured them almost as swiftly as they were produced. I myself am fond of old-fashioned literature. The kind where two chaps smoke their pipes furiously as they pore over an old map. One pulls a bell rope to summon a servant and the other dashes his smoking cap to the carpet. Then they are off in a jumble of cases and portmanteaux to catch the night boat train.

That kind of thing. With engraved illustrations. Gibson girl in high-necked blouse, lips set in a haughty bow, wide eyes, hair piled around a cameo face. And I would be the young man in the high collar leaning anxiously toward her. Just the sort of manly chap who would set off on an impetuous adventure with a chum.

On the hot day when I stopped in the dark bar and heard the man speak of motor oil it was not just to escape the heat.

Someone that certain about motor oil must have firm ideas about other areas of life as well. My first wife did too. She played the piano. A no-nonsense style, firm and precise as her dark eyes. She had been about the age of the young woman hanging on the old guy's arm when she left me. Or I left her. In any event, we separated. Her name was Diana. Oddly romantic name for such a classical lady.

Eventually I had to leave the bar and get in my scorching car and drive to the place where my brother was. I stopped for gas on the way and wouldn't you know that I needed oil? The attendant bent next to the car door to show me the dipstick, his thumb near the add line.

"Ok," I said in what I hoped was a firm, manly tone. "Top it up. Ten w thirty. Any brand you've got."

"We just carry our own," said the attendant.

I had run out of excuses and places to stop so I drove slowly to my brother.

Going down there again a few months later, I felt surges of self pity. It was raining. I had the radio on. I remembered Diana playing *Für Elise*. I remembered an autumn Sunday when our children played in the leaves we were raking. There were layers of leaves, wet down by the frequent rain and a mush of leafmeal under the last layer. It had been a soggy season and now in memory it seemed to me to have been a sad time. It was the autumn before the winter that we split up. Every time I smell apples I remember that time.

Harvest time should be a round-smelling, full, red-gold season. Late boats on the lake, white against the poignant fall blue encourage me. They give a tone of innocent strength to the dying season. Now I had switched stations and the radio played *Cherish* as a golden oldie. It did not seem that old to me.

Boats, I thought. They have a supple strength, a resilient quality which I admire and seem to lack. You don't fool with a boat. It demands. It calls deep and you respond with mingled fear and joy. The boat beckons and you had better leap to the tiller.

I used to sail with Ann, my second wife. I have not been on a boat in years. From a distance, out on the lake they call to me and remind me of what I could be.

The house seemed to get bigger after Diana left me. I kept bumping into myself in the hallways, kept hearing doors open and children call anybody home?

The CAA guide said that there was some Hall of Fame or museum or some damn thing ahead and just off the road. Closed during certain months and also on certain days of the week. But I wanted to make better time to get to where my brother was and could not anyway remember what was the reason for the fame that demanded a building. Baseball? No, that was someplace in New York. Outer Space Pioneers? Inventors of Farm Implements? Maybe Kickboxing or The Discovery of Motor Oil.

I wished I could stop the car and call my father.

Willie died, I would say. *I'm sorry. It's not my fault.* Would those words, the tokens of a child's excuse for anything—coming home past deadline, the lost textbook, the untidied room, the broken promise—serve again for something so big and full of hurt? Would my father's voice, tired but dogged, come through the hollow dark line like a calm beneficence?

And more, could my father offer me a cleansing for all my life's fumbling errors, my whole sad history of meanness and harm? I do not think so.

I drove on in the rain. I have been acquainted with the rain.

Sounds like a quotation. Everything I cherished—or did not love enough—was now gone. I felt I was about to be tested for hardiness and courage. I would be found wanting.

Forgive me I wanted to say to the radio which was in need of the local/distance switch. There was fuzz and static and another station was stepping in and out like a waggish friend putting his head in the door and dodging out again.

I went on down there. Then I placed my brother next to my father and mother. There is room for me there too. But not yet. I have places to go. Perhaps Florence. I want to sleep in a pensione and wake to church bells and music. Someone is playing the piano firmly and with precision. Her teacher is pleased. Someone is wetting down the dust in the pensione's courtyard.

On my way to enplane from Florence someone in white robes proffers a rose. I hesitate. Do I buy it? Flowers are easier to sell. From the plane window I look down on blue water and white boats.

What I was saying before about having this conversation with a woman I hardly knew and there I was *explaining* myself over an inept loud jazz band to someone who was having difficulty hearing me—

I want to become old and bald, powerful and certain.

My daughter called me from California. She had left the community (the term she used) and was living near her mother. Diana is married to a man big in aerospace.

"Mom has really really got it together now," came this voice across the continent.

"Your Uncle Willie died," I said. "You remember him at all?"
"Oh God yes," she said. "Daddy I'm so sorry—"

We talked some more. As soon as she had it together either I would come out there or she would come to me. After we hung up it struck me that she had called me *daddy*. It was a word I had not heard in thirty years. Was it my word of forgiveness? That night I dreamed I heard the sound of children laughing.

A few nights after my daughter's call I dreamed that my

brother was speaking to me. He was on the other side of an expanse of clear water. I could not make out what he said. He spoke in a deeply resonant father's voice. I woke up with it echoing in my ear. Then I wanted to kneel and dig in the autumnal earth to find my brother.

In the movie *Beau Geste* (1939) Digby, one of the three Geste brothers, gives his brother "Beau" (Gary Cooper) a Viking's funeral. This involved setting fire to a Foreign Legion fort. Later on John (Ray Milland) sees his brother Digby (Robert Preston) shot by Arabs.

I cannot erase from my memory the scene in which John hurls himself down a sand dune after his brother's body which rolls to the bottom. In a painfully brief sequence, John's pumping legs send up sprays of sand. I felt that almost falling precipitous rush down the dune in myself. A kind of steep running down, almost falling in my headlong rush after my brother.

The house seemed to expand after Diana's departure, growing baggy like an old sweater morose and loose around me. So also the world seemed to sag and become an aching space after my brother died. It was like being in one of those old railroad stations with preposterously high vaulted ceilings. Why should an ordinary train station take on the grandiose proportions of a medieval cathedral?

I remember being in one years ago at some ridiculous hour— two or three in the morning—waiting for an overdue and inconvenient connection. Nobody was there but me and a sleeping soldier and someone pushing a cleaning cart. A weary amplified voice intoned the half-understood names of cities I never wanted to go to. My brother's passing left me with that same feeling of resigned displacement.

The season turned. Winter came. One night after a movie I walked out to find the Midnite Madness sale in progress. All the downtown merchants were open. Some braved the cold and had tables of merchandise set out on the sidewalks. I went into the dime store. That is not, of course what it is called. There is nothing there that one could purchase for a dime.

And then there among the night shoppers, amid the tables piled with ornaments and trim, the six foot and eight foot artificial trees, it came to me all of a sudden that I did not have to send a Christmas parcel this year. My brother's hands do not need the fur-lined gloves. He does not need his aftershave. I stand there. I cannot think of a thing to do.

My daughter called on Christmas Eve. She has a job working as a researcher for a textbook publisher. She will come to visit me in the spring.

Many people detest telephone answering machines. These purists hang up as soon as they hear the recorded voice. Thus ones machine records an orchestration of bells and clicks and dial tones. I find this frustrating. I will never know who gave up, is now annoyed with me, what good news I will never hear.

But a little while ago my machine recorded something strange. It was not the sound of a hung-up phone. Instead there was a long listening silence. I imagined someone at the other end of the line deliberately filling my machine's tape with the faint, far-off buzz of words not spoken. I had the sinking feeling of imagining the dead trying to connect with the living.

My second wife, Ann, had these crazy dancing evocative eyes. They looked at you hungrily, saying *I'm desperate*. She was fond of New Age music. I always thought her destiny was California. She now lives, however, in Oakville with a lawyer. They are resolutely not married. He has two children by his first marriage. The children (a boy and girl) spend every other weekend with him and Ann. The children have their own room there. A closed toybox waits unused for weeks.

Ann and I foundered on whether or not to have a child. I felt too old but wanted one. My son and daughter from my first marriage are adults. Perhaps I foolishly hoped that a child of our own would make the shaky union with Ann more stable.

Ann chose not to have a child with me. Now she plays the mother to someone else's children every eleven days. I had secretly hoped for a girl. A baby sister for my daughter Carolyn who in fact does not want or need a sister. My son Harry lives not a hour's drive from me and I never hear from him. He has no children.

Then came spring. I remember all the rituals of spring in childhood. I remember rollerskating with my brother. The steel to cement sidewalk thunder. It was a time of tangled string on yo-yos and kites gone up and lost, the kite string fallen over the roofs and yards of strangers.

And I remember one spring when I was a boy and my grandfather took me in his car on an errand. We left the farm and drove on a dirt road for a long time.

Willie, my grandfather said, *We're almost there.*

My grandfather often made a mistake and called me by my brother's name. I did not mind. In a funny way I was made happy by the mistake.

I fell asleep and woke to no motion and the car's engine off. The sun was shining through the opened car window on my hand. I heard the familiar voices of my father, my grandfather, my Uncle Matt and my mother. I was still half asleep and the April sunlight was hot on my hand. I contained it all, my family, the season, that caught moment, forever. I held it in my hand.

April sunshine was calm and warm on my elbow, cocked jauntily on the car's window ledge. From the radio in the car next to me at the stoplight I heard the arpeggios and tremolandi of *Gaspard de la nuit*. I stared at the driver's profile. A woman. Obviously a person of refinement and good taste. She kept her face firmly forward.

I loved the lazy feel of the sun on my arm. It was a sign of the season's rawness and vigour. I wanted to get out of my car and take the hand of the woman in the car next to me. I wanted to waltz with her at the stoplight. The music spoke of Ondine, the lovely water sprite who lured mortal men down to founder in her dark palace deep under the lake's sunny surface. To drown in love. To be one of the company of drowned lovers. The light changed and the woman and the music moved away.

I was not successful in finding the music on my radio. Probably she had been playing a cassette. More evidence of good taste. It was almost time for my car's spring tuneup. The thought filled me with sturdy pleasure. Old worn out oil will be flushed out with all the attendant impurities. New clean oil will bathe my shining valves. I myself felt cleansed in this season of beautiful disorder. It was as if I had taken off a layer of aged skin when I took off my winter coat.

I felt a keen at-oneness with everyone in the world. Seeing people walking down the street looking in store windows filled me with a silly sentimentality. Bashful tears brimmed in my eyes. Was I regressing? I pictured myself at play on a beach. Or perhaps it was my brother on the beach. It is 1939 and he does not know that a war is coming. He builds a crenelated fort in the sand.

Perhaps I have become my brother, kneeling in the sand, carefully making the parapets and battlements with a popsicle stick. Or I became our father, my shoulders slumped with care. Could I go back beyond my father to become his father? I could see myself young and hopeful in another country and century.

I have finished my fort. It will last until the next tide. I look out at boats in a race. They go close-hauled around the buoys. Now my mother is calling to me. It is time to come in for supper. My father has come straight from the office to the cottage. I go up the dune to my mother.

My daughter Carolyn is asleep in my house. She is still catching up with the time changes. She looks thinner than I remember and, naturally, older. But she still has that sweet hesitant smile and look of indefatigable optimism. I, to put it in her words, am getting it together. My daughter has come home. I want to say the word home to the dark window. *Home* is such a reassuring, comforting word.

As I sit staring at the dark window I think I have not understood a single thing that has happened in my life. I went through it like a casual visitor in a museum or a tourist in a theme park. A small bug is bumping against the screen, trying to get in to my light. I look over at the silent telephone. Nobody is trying to get in touch. Where am I? Who calls to me? I am in my house. I am in it.

TERROR EXILE OR DESPAIR

1980

Charles and Shirley O'Neill have just arrived at the Newbolt's after a six hour drive. There is J.B. the eldest child standing on the porch. He is wearing shorts that look like the Maine woods and topsiders with no socks. Charles and Shirley are late. The house is crowded.

"Canada," says Carol Wakefield who has come down the walk to greet them. The Wakefields have lived next door to the Newbolts for twenty years.

"Canada," she says, "Now that's a long way."

"It's just across the river from Detroit," says Shirley.

It seems to Charles that they have had this conversation before, in fact many times over the years. They used to come every summer to visit Shirley's parents who lived in Forest Park. After the parents died, Shirley and Charles continued to come for family reunions. Now Shirley and Mary Ellen are the last of their family. The visits declined and the only connection was the Newbolt Christmas letter.

But this summer the Newbolt children have planned an elaborate surprise twenty-fifth wedding anniversary celebration for their parents. So for the first time in five years Charles and Shirley have made the trip. Charles thinks of the drive to Chicago across Michigan and Indiana the second most boring auto route in North America. The way from Windsor to Toronto wins first prize. But family is family.

Jay Newbolt, Mary Ellen's husband, has always managed to make Charles feel tested, found wanting, second rate. Charles feels that he is constantly explaining himself. Five summers ago he had a kind of argument with Romola Chance (the Chances have lived on the other side of the Newbolts for twenty years) about Vietnam. Romola's bosom was aggressive. It had pointed directly at him like twin cannon. It seemed that Canada was a haven for cowards and draft dodgers. Why didn't Canada have a draft?

"My father was gassed at Ypres," Charles said. "And my Uncle Louie was at Normandy."

None of this had cut any ice with Romola. And now it is Romola herself coming down the walk towards them.

"Well, if it isn't the Canadian cousins," she says.

"Sister," says Shirley who has never liked Romola. Shirley dislikes all big bosomed women on principle.

The Newbolts were among the early settlers in Brookhaven, which grew in the late fifties to rival the population of Winnetka, which lies to the east of it. Brookhaven has risen in status in the past twenty years. There are no sidewalks. Some people have horses. No lot is less than an acre. There are two or three conspicuously up-mobile black families. One of these families, the Wakefields, lives next door. He is a doctor who specializes in allergies.

"Hey there Chuck," says Jack Chance, who comes off the porch and takes Charles by the hand and arm.

Jack is Athletics Director at St. Marcelia's, a small nearby Catholic college. Nobody calls Charles "Chuck." Now Charles feels, as he is heartily walked up the porch steps, like the new ten year old kid on the block. He is being welcomed but also tested. Listen, Chuck, we're going to have a gang. What shall we call our gang? Can you play left field?

J.B. is the most elderly twenty-four year old Charles has ever met. He is named after his father, Jay Brendan. J.B. is the eldest of the five children. He is finishing law school at Northwestern. Three of the other children are at various universities. The two girls, Molly and Wendy are at St. Marcella's. Jason has a football free ride at someplace like Kentucky. Philip, the baby, is still in grade school. Jay senior personally had scouted universities and colleges (all in the Midwest) to find just the right places to fit each child's individual needs.

Charles has always found the Newbolt house aggressive. Like Romola's bosom. The house seemed to make a statement about family and national virtues.

There are blown-up poster sized photos from the wedding hung up. Mary Ellen looks pert, smiling shyly in a rain of flung rice. Jay has a Fifties crewcut. His smile looks too wide for his face. Shirley had been Maid of Honor. There she is, just behind Mary Ellen, seeing to the gown's train. Charles remembers with a pang how beautiful she had been. The wedding was the summer before they met.

Shirley and Mary Ellen grew up in a large West Side Irish family. Shirley once told Charles that all she remembers her relatives talking about was when and exactly where blacks would move in on their neighborhood. They did not, of course, say "blacks."

Mary Ellen, a year older than Shirley, was "the pretty one." Charles wonders why the family made this decision. He has seen family pictures of the two girls at various ages and at first they looked like twins. Only when they reached pubescence did a difference emerge: Mary Ellen was suddenly about two inches taller. But she still didn't seem to have a special edge on pretty.

Shirley said that she didn't remember much about their house on West Washington Boulevard. There was this vividly accurate rendering of the Sacred Heart in the hallway that she had been secretly afraid of. As soon as they could, her parents moved into the suburbs to the west.

Charles is only Irish on his father's side. His mother was French. She was the one who made sure that nobody called him anything but "Charles." His father was something of a bully. He wanted Charles to become a lawyer. When he went into Mechanical Engineering, his father talked seriously about disowning him. Perhaps this is why Charles has never pressured his own children. This is a sore subject between him and Shirley. She says he lacks gumption. Look at Jay, he will say. A martinet. A fascist.

"Hey," says Jay. He is wearing red trousers and a white tee shirt with some kind of tennis emblem on it.

"Where are your kids?" says Jay.

Jason, the second son hands Charles a glass of draft beer. Shirley explains that Cynthia (the Newbolt's goddaughter) has this new job in Toronto and could not possibly take time off, and Steve was already on his way to climb mountains out West when the invitation came. Out West has to be explained to Jack Chance. Yes, Canada has a West too, and Rockies also.

Jay is a tall plump man. He takes Charles by the arm and moves him towards a wall of family photographs. Jay regards the wall in the way he regards the world: he is superior to it and he has a deep conviction that it is his by right.

"It is just remarkable," says Mary Ellen, "How the kids pulled this off. It was really actually a surprise!"

"A real surprise," says Jack Chance.

"Uncle Charles," says Molly, "Have you seen the sequel to *Star Wars* yet?"

Molly is Charles's favorite of the clan. She is a bouncy unsophisticated girl majoring in something called Health Science.

"I don't think it's as good as the first one," Charles says.

"They never are," says Jason, bringing Charles another beer.

Jason is a second string linebacker. Charles is not quite sure where. Is it Kentucky? Charles feels that he is supposed to know and hence cannot ask. Jason's neck is as thick as Charles's thigh. Charles is fond of him.

"Hey there," says Nick Wakefield, "Did these kids do a real secret job or what?"

Now Romola has cornered Charles again. More of the same. When, Charles thinks, will they get over their damned war? He thinks he would like to hurl Romola into the pool.

"On the way here," Charles says to some people on the patio, "We saw this immense beer truck. I mean it was big... and it had *Beer Brewed in God's Country* on it."

Nobody seems to find this as funny as Charles does.

Later on everybody is in the pool, playing a raucous game of waterpolo. Charles plays hard but feels odd man out. New kid on the block business again. Mary Ellen is not in the pool. She is sitting at an umbrella table talking to Connie Quick, who has lived across the street for twenty years. Connie's husband, a big corporate lawyer, dropped dead about six years ago. Forty-seven and in hearty health.

Connie is an ample, slow-moving woman. Blonde of course. From his angle at the pool's edge Charles can see her round thighs under the beige pleated skirt. She stretches her torso as she leans in to listen to Mary Ellen. Shirley is sitting with them. The Widder Quick, Charles had joked five years before. Shirley had not thought it was funny. The Widow Quick had seemed far too flirty and danced with too many men (including Charles) on that occasion.

Back at the motel, late, Charles feels keyed up. The motel is in Millrace Acres, a less fancy suburb to the south of Brookhaven. Charles watches cable tv with the sound down so Shirley can sleep.

They always stay at this motel when they visit. It is a strange sort of place. It never seems full. Nobody ever is in the pool. There is no coffee shop. Shirley calls it the Bates Motel. Charles says they probably do ok during the week with business travelers. There are religious and inspirational books on a rack near the front desk.

Charles is watching a Bruce Lee movie. The one set in Rome where gangsters are trying to take over Bruce's uncle's restaurant.

Just before they left the party, Charles had seen Jay talking to Connie near the poolhouse. Mary Ellen and Shirley were at the umbrella table, deep in a sister's colloquy. There was something intent about Jay and Connie. Something, Charles thinks now as he watches Bruce Lee fight someone in the Coliseum, something private. Furtive.

Or was it all the booze and all the talking and horseplay that put him in this paranoid frame of mind? The Newbolts and Chances and all their crowd were vigorously straight-arrow. Why young J.B. even defended Nixon, saying that all sorts of things would come out about the Kennedys. History would give Nixon justice in time.

Before he turns in Charles lifts the curtain to look out at the open field which slopes down from the motel to a cinderblock building. They drive past it on the way to and from the motel. It is a place where people board their dogs when they go on vacation. As one passes the place, one hears the incessant chorus of barking howling and whimpering.

There is a celebratory Mass at noon the next day. J.B. is

asked by the priest to speak for the family after the homily. J.B. gives a rather moving and succinct tribute to his parents and also manages to say something nice about each of his siblings.

The church is much older than Brookhaven. It formerly served several generations of German farmers. After Mass, everyone mills around in front. Jack Chance is yelling over Charles's shoulder at someone. Something about who is riding with who. There will be a luncheon on the Newbolt patio. Charles and Shirley checked out earlier so they can start for home after lunch.

The benign sun filtered through the trees that flanked the patio. It was sit-down and catered. Bottles of red and white wine were on each table. Shirley and Charles sat with Connie and Kelly, a school friend of Wendy's. Charles looked over at the bigger table where Jay and Mary Ellen were bracketed by their children and the priest who was now wearing a golf tee shirt.

This whole thing, Charles thought, was one of those rites of passage moments in life. In two years it will be Charles and Shirley's twenty-fifth. He wonders if Steve and Cynthia will plan something.

They are the first to leave. Jay and Mary Ellen walk out to the car with them. Jay gives Charles directions that will save a lot of time getting to the interstate. Charles pretends to listen. He is going to go the way he always does. He is certain of that route and is reluctant to embark on the unknown.

Then they are on their way. Shirley says well, it was very nice. Yes, says Charles, it was a very nice occasion.

1990

Charles and Shirley are driving past the dog boarding place. The animal's hullabaloo rises and falls behind them. They have come back for the first time since the twenty-five year party. This time it is for a somber reason. Molly has died of leukemia. The Christmas letters stopped four years ago, when Jay told Mary Ellen that he wanted a divorce, that he had never loved her and that he wanted a chance for both of them to have a new life.

Now Jay and Connie are married and live in Winnetka. Mary Ellen is still in the big house, but now that Philip has finished high school she will begin to look for something smaller and maybe not in Brookhaven.

J.B. is calling himself Brendan these days. He has accepted and embraced his ethnic roots. He and his wife Candy have a child, Deirdre, the first Newbolt grandchild. Wendy is married, but so far no children. All the children live in Brookhaven or close by. They seem to have coped with the breakup. They spend Christmas Eve with Mary Ellen and have dinner with their father the next day. They seem to have accepted Connie. Jack Chance died in 1983. Romola has moved to Ohio to be near her daughter who lives in Shaker Heights.

Rumors had found their way to Charles and Shirley in the past decade. Wendy had an abortion and gave up her scholarship at Loyola to follow her lover to Alaska. Or was it Iowa? The lover was older and married. Or younger and black. Was any of this true? All they knew for sure was that Wendy is now married, is not at Loyola and is living somewhere in or near Brookhaven.

Jason gave up his Big Eight football free ride to go into a seminary. He left that and finished his degree at a close-to-home college. Now he is in the quality control end of his father's plant.

With all this and the divorce, Charles and Shirley think their own family is dull normal. Steve is married and lives near Toronto. They phoned just before Charles and Shirley left for the trip to tell them that Michelle, Steve's wife, is pregnant. Cynthia is not married. She teaches elementary school in Windsor. She was engaged but broke it off. She isn't seeing anybody seriously right now.

At the funeral parlor Jay stands near the foot of the casket. The coffin is closed. A framed photo of Molly is on the coffin. Brendan stands on one side of his father and Wendy on the other. Connie is sitting in the front row, talking to a young woman holding a child. Charles assumes that this is Brendan's wife and baby. Mary Ellen stands near the head of the casket.

Philip stands next to her. She looks old and shrunken. Shirley embraces her and they stand like that for a moment. Charles, standing behind Shirley, nods gravely to Brendan. Jay, who is talking to Nick Wakefield, has not seen them yet.

Now Charles puts his arms around Mary Ellen says *I'm so sorry, so sorry.* She feels like a cage of spun glass in his arms. Then he stands next to her. Shirley stands next to Philip on the other side. Old friends approach, hesitate, then go to either Jay or Mary Ellen to express their condolences. There seems to be no pattern to the choosing of which parent will be solaced first.

So fragile a thing life is, Charles thinks. Fragile as love. Terror exile despair. Something he read in a literature course a long time ago. Something about our mortality. Something to say against the dark. Otherwise it would be like the helpless yowling of abandoned pets at the shelter.

Who has abandoned us? Left us here crying in the dark? The baby, now held on Connie's lap, begins to cry. Mary Ellen goes over to Connie, bends down. Connie holds up the child for her to take. Mary Ellen holds the baby up on her shoulder crooning to it, making soft soothing sounds. It is a posture Charles remembers, when Mary Ellen and Shirley held and comforted their babies. Something he thinks, eternal in the act, timeless. It seems to him now that it transcends even the fury that must have existed between Mary Ellen and Connie.

The priest arrives. Everyone sits down. Mary Ellen, Shirley and Philip are on the left. Mary Ellen still holds the child. Jay and the other children are on the right. The priest reads the prayers. The responses are on laminated cards, like menus. Then the priest gives a brief homily. He says he only got to know Molly in these last weeks but he has grown to admire her courage and deep faith which should be a powerful example to us who are left behind.

After the prayers, the funeral director asks the pallbearers to meet with him for a moment before leaving. On the way out Charles pauses to look at a collage of family snapshots on a bulletin board featuring Molly at various ages. There is one where she is about three and there is Shirley in the background talking to Steve who appears to be upset about something.

Charles realizes that he has not yet spoken to Jay nor to his new wife. Now he stands in the vestibule of the funeral parlor. It is raining. Charles wonders what would be the proper thing to do. Awkward to go back in. They are closing the place. Jay must be very tired. Charles hold the door for Shirley. They are going back to the big house for coffee or a drink with Mary Ellen.

"They should have asked you to be a pallbearer," says Shirley. "After all I was Molly's godmother."

"Well," says Charles, adjusting the wiper speed, "Remember that they didn't ask me to be godfather. Who was her godfather anyhow?"

"Jack Chance," says Shirley.

"Sure," says Charles. "Of course."

At the big house Shirley has coffee. Charles asks for scotch and soda. There isn't any soda. Plain water will be fine Charles says.

They sit out next to the pool. The rain has let up.

"Phil cleans it every day," says Mary Ellen, "But nobody uses it anymore."

"It's something they outgrow," says Shirley.

Charles looks at the dark still water and thinks of the drunken yelling crowd splashing and laughing. A maudlin memory. Jack Chance, big and alive. Romola carrying her prejudices like a fierce banner. Molly on the diving board pretending to throw and then holding back the ball. Connie at the poolside table talking to the woman she was even then planning to betray.

Gone, all gone. He looks up at the dark and silent house. Soon strangers will live in it. Perhaps they will be younger and full of hope. Their children will love the pool. The water will be roiled and showers of flung water will be caught in sunlight.

Charles remembers Steve staying in too long at some motel pool, climbing out, shivering, his lips blue, to be covered with a towel by Shirley. Fun, taken to excess, like too much candy at a carnival. Too much to drink at a party. Young, old, we all crowd to the pleasure of the moment.

The rain stops early in the morning but the sky is still overcast. The ground in the cemetery is soggy. Carpets of artificial grass have been laid around the gravesite. By the time Charles and Shirley get out of their car and make it up a sloping hill, the priest is already starting the prayers. He sprinkles holy water on the coffin. Brendan steps forward and lays a single white rose on the coffin. Now the priest speaks quietly to Jay and Mary Ellen who stand next to one another but apart.

People begin to drift back down the slope to the cars. Some have left their headlights on. Shirley and Charles are not going back to Jay and Connie's for the lunch. They are heading out for home right away. Shirley hugs Mary Ellen. Then they get in the car and head toward the cemetery gates.

After they get on the I-94 the clouds begin to break up. As they cross the Indiana line the sun comes full out. Shirley puts a K.T Oslin tape on. They have become country&western fans. Shirley says something. Charles answers *hmmm?* He does this all the time now. Shirley says he sounds like Citizen Kane talking to his second wife. Charles is getting more and more hard of hearing but puts off going to be tested for a hearing aid.

The muffler falls down and bangs and thumps the concrete. They slow down and exit near Portage. They drive towards a tall Esso sign. When they get to it, the station is closed up. It looks as if it has been closed for a long time. Why don't they take the damn sign down says Charles. The muffler thumps and scrapes along. How can a road be so long without a single gas station.

Then they are suddenly in a small town and there is a garage with a big sign *We Fix Mufflers.* It is not a muffler chain. On the right of the garage is a pristine lake, sparkling in the sun.

The mechanic says their car is Canadian so he has no mufflers to fit. Something about emission laws. But he can weld a straight pipe on. It will get them home. It will cost fifteen dollars. Shirley walks down to look at the lake.

"Canada," says the mechanic as the car rises on the hoist. "That's real pretty up there. I've seen pictures."

On the way back to the interstate Charles feels an eye-smarting benevolence towards all of America. The small town, the pure and shining lake, the honest mechanic. He will tell people about it whenever there is anti-American talk.

It is dark when they stop to eat in Michigan. And there is a long line-up on the bridge. A lot of people have been over shopping and are making declarations. The customs inspector looks skeptical when Charles tells him that they have nothing to declare, that they have been at a funeral. The inspector sends them over to have the car searched. Charles feels justifiable outrage.

They have been on the road for a long time. The muffler thing and the customs hangup have not helped. He brings the bags in but they decide not to unpack until tomorrow. Charles brings two glasses of wine out to the screened-in porch. The summer is really over Shirley says. Yes, Charles says, you can really feel a change in the air.

After awhile Charles goes in to catch the late news. Shirley stays out on the porch. A car drives past, slowly, as if searching for an address. She watches the tail lights go down the block. She remembers Cynthia and Molly as babies. Maybe Steve and Michelle's child will be a girl. She does not want to say this out loud. Something Irish keeps her from forming a final wish about the baby, keeps her from hoping too much. She will buy yellow baby clothes. She imagines a baby sleeping on her lap.

She remembers a time when she and Mary Ellen were little, about six and seven. They had been playing under the dining room table and their parents were sitting at the table, talking. Shirley remembers the feeling of peace and enclosure. The lace tablecloth hanging all around like a veil. Her father's voice, her mother's voice. Quiet, ordinary words. And being there, with her sister, feeling safe.

Maybe that was the very last time she ever felt that safe. Now she rises to go in to sit with her husband to see what the weather will be like tomorrow.

There has been another drive-by shooting across the river. Another child killed by mistake. Charles thinks about his grandchild to be. For some reason he pictures it as a girl. He will not say this out loud. The high pressure ridge that has been hanging around the Great Lakes for so long is finally moving to the east. It looks pretty good for tomorrow. Heat wave in Arizona. Rain in Tennessee. Flooding in Calgary. Fire out of control in California. But finally it looks as if a better day is coming our way.

1956

Charles has had three interviews since graduation. One with Ford, one with GM and one with the C.D. Bucke Company. Things look promising. The Bucke outfit is fairly new. They do parts for the big three. Bucke seems to Charles to offer the most challenge. He is off now to Chicago for a final interview at head office.

On the train he sits with two girls who are on their way home after visiting a school friend in Ann Arbor. One of the girls is pregnant. That's ok, because Charles fancies the other one, who looks like Leslie Caron in *An American in Paris.*

The train rolls across Michigan and Indiana. Charles is happy. The job seems to be a sure thing. This girl sitting across from him, smiling, is really first class. And then, finally, there are the towers of Chicago, shining in the late slant of sunlight. He has the girl's phone number in his wallet. Anything, everything, could happen.

THE SURGICAL PROCEDURE

It was in Chicago, at Kinsley's restaurant. Augustus St. Gaudens looked around the table and said "Gentlemen, this is the greatest meeting of artists since the Fifteenth Century." It was 1891. The artists included, besides St. Gaudens, architects Daniel Burnham and Richard Hunt, the painter Frank D. Millet and two popular sculptors, Frederick William MacMonnies and Daniel Chester French.

Why, thought Anthony, did so many of them have three names? He began to type again.

They were in Chicago to plan for the World Columbian Exposition which was to open two years later. Even if St. Gaudens may have been yielding to a surge of egotism, there was a lot of talent gathered at that table.

However, there was one man absent from the lunch. Adam Willis Chambers, friendly rival to both St. Gaudens and French, had died suddenly eleven years earlier at the age of forty-nine. During the latter part of the Seventies his work was almost as popular as theirs and in that period when public sculpture flourished, bronze Civil War generals, statesmen, memorials, allegorical fountains in parks by Chambers were unveiled at what seems to us today an almost hectic pace.

Anthony stopped again. It all seemed so thin, general, insubstantial, bookish. Dry. Now, in the photographs of August Sander, people looked like what they were: musicians, businessmen, judges, soldiers, farmers, pastry cooks, circus workers. A maitre d' looked arrogant. The composer Paul Hindemith looked like a composer. It was as if they had been assigned roles and then shaped each respective physiognomy to suit.

Anthony was no expert on the photography of August Sander. He was not an expert on anything. But as Editor, Publisher and sole proprietor of *Heirloom*, a monthly journal of art and antiques, he learned a little about a lot. Now he knew a little more about Adam Willis Chambers, planned feature of the following month's issue.

Adam Willis Chambers. b. 1831. d. 1880. Corporal, USA, 1862-65. Studied sculpture, Paris, 1866-70. First commission,

1871: *Flora,* ornamental figure for Berman Block, Rye, N.Y. Married Madeline Lovell, 1872. No children.

Anthony stared at the three by five card. It was all so tantalizingly barren of life, blood, the real thing.

A clue; When Chambers died, his widow tried to set up a foundation and an artist's colony. She had scant success and had to abandon the project. Sketches for the abandoned plan were among what she called The Chambers Papers, left to the Society For the Preservation of the Beaux Arts when she died in 1925.

The Society was located in a three storey building on the Near North Side. The library reminded Anthony of the Thatcher Library in *Citizen Kane.* The security guard managed to look aloof, contemptuous, suspicious and vicious. The Chambers Papers was a cardboard box full of letters, paid receipts from 1902, religious pamphlets, school reports from Madeline's youth, warranties on electric appliances from the early Twenties and a copy of Adam Willis Chambers's will.

Chambers must have lived high, Anthony thought, because despite all the popularity he died almost destitute. Poor Madeline must have had a bad time of it. There was one puzzling bequest. *Head of Cupid.* Bronze medallion, left to one Stephanie Harding.

Anthony knew that Stephanie had been the model he used most often in the important commissions. She was "Psyche" in *Arcadia*, a group on top of the Mercantile Building in Hartford. She was all the caryatids on the Cheney Bank in Portsmouth. She was "Dawn" in *The Dance of the Hours*, a fountain in front of a library in Illinois. Why had Chambers left her this medallion? Surely she had not been the model for Cupid. If not, who had?

Anthony had dinner with Norma, his ex-wife, once a week. It was part of their amiable divorce. (His first, her second as they say in *Time* magazine.)

"On the way here I saw a bumper sticker," Anthony said. "Smite. For God Loves You."

"I've seen that," said Norma, "I think you need glasses. It's *smile* not smite."

"I think my version is better," said Anthony.

"Why are you so interested in this—what's his name?" said Norma.

She was mixing a salad. She always added too much lemon juice and not enough garlic. Anthony liked it on the dry side. Anthony tended to judge Norma too detachedly he thought.

"It's complicated," he said. "Here. Let me do the garlic."

"Many things seem to be complicated for you," she said.

Lately she had been given to such cryptic remarks.

"He was an important person in his own time," Anthony said. "An artist who was also a public success."

"I think you like him because he's dead," said Norma. "Aren't you overdoing that garlic?"

"Keeps vampires away," said Anthony.

"You do garlic press so well," she said. "With the skill of a surgeon. The garlic surgical procedure. You should have been a surgeon."

Anthony was to remember this conversation.

Stephanie Harding had moved to St. Louis in 1879. She died in 1935. Initially she had continued her modeling, appearing in various guises on the covers of *Century* and *Scribners* until about 1901 when she retired and opened a restaurant. Maxfield Parrish was alleged to have done a mural for the restaurant which was in a building demolished in 1946.

Anthony learned a lot from the papers left by Stephanie to the Society For American Sculpture. They weren't called "papers" and the Society's offices had none of the stilted grandeur of the Beaux Arts library. There was an unfinished memoir, in Stephanie's hand. It was mostly about her St. Louis days. There were letters written by Chambers addressed to her. Mainly these contained complaints about parsimonious clients and inept foundry assistants.

Some, however, admonished Stephanie on treatments for various childhood diseases. What had their relationship been?

There was no record of Stephanie ever marrying. There were other letters, beginning "Dear Mother" and signed "Adam."

Anthony felt a thrill of discovery. The trail of Chambers life had led from Chicago to St. Louis and here almost a hundred years later, his guilt was held up in the afternoon light coming in the windows, held in Anthony's hands.

Adam's letters to his mother indicated that he had left home in 1903, married one Ellen Maltman in New Orleans in 1915, divorced her in Kansas City in 1920. He married Ruth Urquart in 1922 in Chicago and divorced her in that same city in 1928. Then he married Jean Quinn in 1929 and did not divorce her—at least by 1935 when Stephanie died and the letters stopped.

There was issue from this final union. Baxter Harding was born in Chicago in 1930. So Stephanie had a grandchild and Adam Willis Chambers had a direct descendent. The trail led back to Chicago.

Anthony's search of old city directories showed the Hardings living on the West Side until Adam Jr's death. Then the widow and her son moved to LaGrange Hills, a suburb some twenty miles further west. Baxter was drafted, a check of army records showed, in 1953 but was not sent to Korea. In 1955, he enrolled at the University of Illinois Chicago Undergraduate Division. He did not complete a degree. His mother died in 1959. Now he was living a scant five or six blocks away from Anthony and owned his own interior decorator's shop. He was in the phone book.

Detective work, Anthony thought, dialing the number was ridiculously easy. The movies, as usual, had it all wrong.

"I really don't know all that much about my grandfather," said Baxter. His voice was deep and petulant. "I mean he died so long ago. My father talked about him like somebody famous you might have met for five minutes sometime or other. I think he died before my father was old enough to remember."

"Well," Anthony said, staring out the office window at the elevated train turning the curve. The late sun flashed off the train windows.

"I don't really know how much I need to know," Anthony went on. "More I mean. About all I have is this family, uh, connection and I'm not sure it fits in with all the rest of the article. I mean *Heirloom* is about art, really, not about people."

"Maybe it could go in *People*." the deep voice laughed. "*People* magazine I mean. Listen, why not come for tea this Sunday. I'll dig up what I can. I still do have that bronze. Quite handsome. I think the Beaux Arts are due for a revival."

"Well that's so kind of you, hate to impose—"

"About fourish," said Baxter. "I'll be away until Sunday morning and is four ok?"

Anthony made more civilized noises and hung up. What more did he need? *Heirloom* wasn't a gossip mag. He already had more than enough on Chambers the artist. He looked at the photos which would accompany the article. *The Head of Cupid, Sleeping Nymph, The Fountain of the Ages* complete with festoons, cherubs, sea horses, spouting dolphins, maidens simpering, some holding wreaths, or cornucopias. My god, due for a revival. Antique dealers take notice: Depression glass out, Beaux Arts in.

Anthony looked around his cramped little office. It could pass for a private eye's office, all grimy windows and worn furniture and clutter. All it lacked was the faithful secretary.

He hadn't seen Norma in two weeks. The trip to St. Louis. Cheap excuses. In Bergman's *Wild Strawberries* in one of the humiliating dream sequences, Alman, the inquisitor, shows Dr. Borg a vision of his long dead wife.

Then Alman says "She is gone. Everybody is gone. Everything has been dissected. A surgical masterpiece. There is no pain, no bleeding, no quivering."

Norma often quoted those lines to Anthony. And he knew what the next bit of dialogue was. Borg asks what his punishment will be and Alman answers simply loneliness.

Sunday was a bright, cold day. Anthony spent a bit of time fussing over his notes. He really had too much information, unless he wanted to attempt a full scale book on Chambers.

What a strange world it had been a hundred years ago. Great wealth and poor taste. Flamboyance. Well, Anthony thought, maybe not so different from today. People are still uneasy about art. They buy somebody else's taste.

President Cleveland opens the Columbian Exposition. Poem by Richard Watson Gilder on the Exposition: "Ah! Happy West. Greece flowers anew and all her temples soar!" Three names again. He looked at a photo of Chambers in someplace where something was being cast. A short, dandyish figure, with a small pointed beard and rimless eye glasses. He wore a slouch hat, like the one Whitman wore for the first edition of *Leaves of Grass.* Light glinted on the glasses. The eyes of the artist. Eyes of a lecher. Lecherous artist. Artistic lecher.

Baxter Harding's apartment was north of Foster, near Broadway. Just past Farragut Street. *Farragut*: statue done by Chambers's colleague, St. Gaudens. Then past Willow Street which was hardly more than an alley. It was the kind of street that decorators and artists and people who liked to live close to artists lived on. Quaint and so on. No, he didn't want to attempt a full scale bio of Chambers. What was he doing here on this fool's errand?

A half block from Baxter's place, a group of people crowded around something out in the street. Anthony walked closer. It was two, no three, people lying in a heap. They were all bleeding. Nobody in the group standing there seemed to be doing anything. Nobody said anything.

"What happened?" Anthony asked.

"Hit and run," said a red faced man wearing a knitted hat. "Lady and two kids. She tried to shield them, looks like."

"Anybody call an ambulance?" Anthony asked. "I don't know," the man in the knitted hat said. " I was out jogging and saw the crowd. I just got here myself."

"Did anybody call an ambulance?" Anthony said to a large woman with an impassive face who pretended not to hear.

Anthony ran back down the street to a store. He asked the owner to call the police. He asked the owner if be had a blanket or something to cover the people with.

"Blanket?" the man said. He had a long unsmiling face. "Look, this is a *candy* store. I don't have blankets."

He didn't look like the kind of man who should be running a candy store.

But then, Anthony thought as he walked quickly back to the scene, that crabby kind always seem to run candy stores. Now he heard sirens. Maybe somebody in one of the houses had called for help. The bleeding bodies hadn't moved. Subject for a Chambers group. *Medea and Her Children.* Something artfully pathetic. White marble, no blood. No awkward clothes all bloody and twisted around. An ambulance turned into the street.

Anthony went on. He felt agitated, queasy, absurdly guilty. But what could he have done? He wasn't a doctor. It was unreasonable, but the feeling persisted.

The way to Harding's apartment was through a garden gate, down a path overgrown with bushes and then down a damp passageway and *then* through another back yard, completely closed in by buildings. There was no way in from the front. It was a kind of half basement. Small windows faced on sidewalk level. The door was ajar.

Anthony knocked. There was no answer. He knocked harder and the door swung in. Just like a private eye movie. Now somebody would attack him.

"Come in, come *in* for godssake," said a voice.

"Look at this mess," a tall man in a tan sweater said, gesturing around at what really was a mess. Books, furniture, crockery, framed pictures, a large Chinese vase, records were all scattered around the room.

"Ripoff bastards. It's not enough that they take the damn TV and all the money they can find. They have to wreck the fucking place—"

He was so angry that he stammered. His face was flushed and he hadn't yet looked directly at Anthony.

"Look," said Anthony, "Let me help you straighten—"

"Oh shit," sighed the man. "You must be whatshisname from the magazine."

"I could come back another time," said Anthony, "Mr.—"

"Call me Bax. God! Little ripoff swine. It's neighborhood kids. They need the money for drugs. I should move someplace safer, but where is *that*?"

They both began moving around the room, righting the chairs, picking up unbroken stuff. Harding rehung pictures, adjusting them at arm's length. Anthony set the tall Chinese vase back on its pedestal table and propped up the dried weeds that he surmised had been in it.

"To hell with tea," said Harding. "Let's have some wine. Sorry I don't have anything stronger."

"This has been a strange day," Anthony said. "I saw this terrible accident a block from here. Now this. It's like the world is falling apart."

"Anybody hurt?" Harding called from the kitchen. He came back into the room with a bottle of wine, which he put between his knees and worked in the corkscrew.

"I don't know," Anthony said. "They weren't moving. Lot of blood—"

"What?"

"Blood."

"Oh. Well, here's the wine," said Harding, holding out a glass. "Cheap. Not distinguished. Plonk. Not even naughty. Just basic."

They sat on a small green couch.

"Here's to my illustrious grandfather," said Harding, raising his glass. "From what my father used to say, my grandmother must have been been a saint. Or a martyr. Knew a lot of artists— the—besides my grandfather I mean—the famous illustrators? But my father's stories were really, really strange. He'd talk about happy life in St. Louis and the famous restaurant and then tell a story sounded like this orphan in Dickens. He was lots older than my mother."

"Shouldn't you call the police?" said Anthony.

"Yes, and the insurance company," said Harding. "I know the whole routine now. But no rush. There is no way they'll catch the little pricks."

Harding got up and went into another room. Anthony looked around. They had done a pretty fair job of cleaning up. It was a very pleasant room with the late sun coming in through the little windows over the sidewalk.

"Here is the bronze," Harding said, holding it up in the light.

It was larger than Anthony had imagined.

"Handsome," he said. "Really marvelous. You know, you can almost sense that he really loved the boy—there's a sort of tenderness there—"

"Yes," Harding said, propping the medallion against a wall. "And there are these papers and all. Letters. Bunch of *restaurant* receipts. Deeds to places my parents lived. Why do people save this crap?"

"I saw the things your grandmother left to the Society in St. Louis," Anthony said.

"Here," said Harding, holding out the bottle and shaking it a little, "Let me top that up for you. St. Louis. I should go down there sometime. I'm really not all that curious though. Suppose I ought to be. Roots and all. Was there anything there about my grandfather's death? Cause of death I mean? Dying young like that—"

"No," Anthony frowned in concentration. "I don't remember anything—"

"I have this odd fear that I'm going to die young," Harding said. He was smiling as he said it. Anthony could not be sure how serious he was.

"Tainted blood or something," Harding kept on smiling. "I do have this condition. They've run all sorts of tests but nothing certain yet. The doctor said something about maybe a surgical 'procedure' maybe. But maybe it skips a generation. My father lived a long time. But I guess I'd better hope for skipping two generations— Are you married?"

"No," Anthony laughed a little. "Not anymore."

"I'm not either. Ever, I mean. And no children. Where will the next generation come from," said Harding. "You know, my father told me—this was right before he died—I was just a kid, didn't understand. Anyway, he heard they were tearing down a whole area in New York and he went there on the train—sat up all night—because there was this statue in an alcove over a doorway—one of the famous buildings—statue of—anyway, by *my* grandfather. Female figure. Suppose he thought—my father I mean—that my grandmother might have modelled for it. I think he meant to take a picture or maybe get a piece of it broken off—souvenir? But when he got there, all he did was stand and watch the wrecker's ball slam into it. Just stood there watching. I imagined it looking like that lady on the box of cornstarch all exalted and old timey? Anyhow, then he just caught the next train home."

"What a strange story," said Anthony. "I wonder why he did that?"

"Who knows why people do anything," Harding sighed. "Listen. It's getting late—"

"Yes," said Anthony, looking around for a place to put his glass down. "I mustn't take anymore of your time—"

"No, I was going to suggest sending for a pizza. I didn't have time to go shopping yesterday. Even if I had, it would all be smeared on the kitchen floor. Why not take potluck? Here. Just a teardrop in the bottle. I'll get another—"

Anthony made protesting noises, but he was hungry, a little more than light-headed and reluctant to get up. Harding went to the phone and dialed a number he knew by heart, and gave detailed instructions on how to find his place. He repeated the instructions. He had just replaced the phone in its cradle when it rang.

"Yes," he said. "Well, I've been here and the phone simply has not rung. The neighborhood bullies have broken in again. No. Broken in. Stole the tv again. But it's the *mess*. The mess. Can't you hear? No. I'll call you. Tomorrow. *Tomorrow*. Yes. All right. You too."

"God," he said, gesturing at the phone after he had hung it up again. "People. Intruders. In trud ers. Break in on your place and your life—"

"They even invade the privacy of your body," he went on

from the kitchen. "Thank God the little bastards aren't fond of wine. Let me top that up. Intruders. Get into your fucking blood-stream. Somebody you did not even ever *know*—"

Harding came back into the room and switched on a lamp. Then he began a long story which Anthony had difficulty following. Seemed it took place right after Harding got out of the army. When he was a student. It involved this music student he had met. From Northwestern. In Evanston. Music student lived there. How he, Harding, went up there often on the subway?

Anyhow. This *music* student had the soul of a gnat. Betrayed him with a little turd of a pipsqueak. Harding was crying. Tears ran down his cheeks.

"I don't want to die," he said. "I haven't even lived yet."

Someone was at the door. It was the pizza. Anthony tried to pay for half but Harding would have none of that.

"I specifically said 'no anchovies' but these people have minds of their own," Harding said, laying out paper napkins.

"Oh I should call the police," he went on in an undertone mumble. "Not that they'll do anything. Routine bullshit. But I need it for the insurance people."

"You know," said Anthony, suddenly convinced, "I don't think I'm going to touch this personal angle in the article. "Who *really* wants to know and all?"

"People love the inside scoop," Harding sighed, lifting a slice of drooping pizza to his mouth with both hands. "Never mind the pain, the personal grief and all—"

Anthony sipped his wine while Harding phoned the police. "Said they'd be right out. Ha. Last time it was three hours."

Harding sat down with a thump. He began to cry again and somehow Anthony had his arm around him and Harding was sobbing against his shoulder. Over Harding's head he could see the *Head of Cupid*, lamplight throwing the child's face into relief. It did look tender. Poor boy. Poor Chambers. Poor Stephanie.

And poor Baxter. Inheritor of all. Anthony made soothing noises.

They went into the kitchen and made some coffee. "I'll definitely call you," Anthony said at the door. "And I'll send you a copy of the issue when it comes out."

"I should subscribe," Harding called. "In my business and all—"

Anthony stumbled on the steps.

"Careful out there," Harding called. "It's an insane place. Really should move out—"

"OK," Anthony called back. "Kind of charming. The place I mean—"

Anthony felt his way through the passageway and out through the little garden and into dimly lit Willow Street Crescent. He headed south. No intruders. No accident victims in the street. People breaking and entering. Jumping into your life like paratroopers. Commandos with knives in their teeth. Knives like scalpels.

Who intruded on who. Whom. Anthony felt that he had not ever intruded on anybody's space. California word. He felt like a passerby, an Editor, a Critic, a Detective, an impassive Surgeon—

Adam Willis Chambers now, he had lived. He had caused— maybe was causing—pain. But his life had been passionate a hundred years ago.

Hundred years was not quaint and far off. You could reach out and touch it in the dark. He stopped and looked back down the empty street. He could almost fancy Chambers standing down there as he stood in his slouch hat in the foundry. Anthony had an absurd impulse to bow or wave— somehow acknowledge the presence.

Adam Chambers was no mere dandy in an old photograph. Caused pain? Herman Melville's son shot himself. What happened to Gauguin's children? Bach's? What was it made it so tough for the children of artists? Did Mozart have children?

Baxter Harding did not, Anthony thought, nor do I. And I have not his excuse. Slowly, humbled, Anthony bowed towards the dark street. Just as slowly, he imagined, the dim figure in the slouch hat down there returned his salute. Then Anthony turned and went on his way.

THE LIFE AND DEATH OF THE FIEND
HENRY H. HOLMES

"I went one evening into a dressing-room in the twilight," said Henry James, "To procure some article that was there; when suddenly there fell upon me, without any warning, just as if it came out of the darkness, a horrible fear of my own existence."

Darwin said somewhere that the suffering of the lower animals throughout time was more than he could bear to think of. So, let us not think of it. We can do what we will with the past. Living at the pinnacle of history, we look back with smugness. It is like looking at a mural in a large public building, all spread out in bold heroic colours, totally known.

Broadhatted pioneers gaze serenely westward, statuesque women stand bravely next to them, the painted continent is ready to be traversed. But Henry H. Holmes's world was different. Lower class brutes in derby hats jostled on the sidewalk next to bustled demure matrons and spade-bearded swells in top hats. It was a time of gaslit horror, giving way to the wonder of electricity.

Henry Holmes was born when the Civil War began. He died before World War One. Disappointed, he dreamed of battles. The air thick with murderous iron, the shouts and screams of the wounded. He saw himself as an officer, weeping alone in his tent over his fallen troops, secretly having it off as he dreamed of necrophiliac sex.

He was tried for the murder of Ben Pitezel in Philadelphia. Found guilty, he was hanged in 1896. He confessed that he had killed one hundred and thirty-seven people. Gossip in Chicago put the number of victims up to two hundred.

Ironically, he was probably not guilty of the murder of Ben Pitezel. Holmes was buried in an over-sized grave ten feet deep. The coffin was filled with cement to prevent the possibility of an outraged citizenry's posthumous revenge.

Licentious Joys

He killed his best friend when they were both eleven years old. Later on he murdered a classmate at the University of Michigan Medical School. It was part of an insurance fraud scheme. He married a girl named Clara, had a child, abandoned both. Never bothering to divorce Clara, he married many times afterwards. He did not finish medical school. But he had learned to dissect.

How he loved to dissect! Cutting up a corpse was almost as pleasurable as murder or enjoying after-killing sex on his female victims.

Shipwrecked On The Shoals Of Honour

"Will you please pardon my addressing myself to you in this manner?" he said in his deep resonant firm melodious voice.

Holmes and the young girl were sitting in the drawing room of his house. It was filled with cut velvet chairs, red velvet drapes, ostrich feathers in cloisonné vases, gilt-framed landscapes and studies of large-eyed girls clutching small animals. A parlour organ stood on one wall.

The Veteran Debauchee

Holmes had designed the building himself. The property was on the south side of Chicago near the railroad. He took many train rides in his career. As construction had proceeded, Holmes fired and hired workmen, architects and flunkies. Thus nobody knew the whole labyrinthine scheme of the place except Holmes himself. It was a maze of tunnels, secret trapdoors, secret rooms, peepholes, a quicklime pit in the cellar and a room for Henry's dissecting expertise.

"I scarcely think it is due to over-sensitiveness on my part," he went on slowly, "That you have seemed of late to repel me. Had I not previously been made gratefully happy by your frank cordiality I should unquestionably accept your present manner as indicative of your wishes in regard to me and my feelings."

Holmes was mindful of the lessons he had learned so well from *The Popular Elocutionist*. Love had to be approached with the utmost delicacy. It was best expressed by a deep, fervent and impassioned tone of voice. Placing the right hand over the heart was advised. Should he evoke the "languishing eyes" routine? It could border on burlesque. Better to use the steady respectful gaze.

HOLMES THE ARCHITECT

Holme's house was extensive. There were thirty-five rooms on the second floor. A special furnace had been installed in the cellar, capable of great heat. The inventor of the furnace was the first victim to be incinerated.

RAPTURE: THE FATAL ENCOUNTER

He had keen, snapping electric blue eyes. He was able to convince young women of his sincerity in a very brief period of time. Jennie had come to Chicago from a small town in Southern Illinois in order to find a job. Henry offered her one, and now moved from prospective employer to lover.

"If I have offended you in any way," he went on, "It has been unknowingly. With this in view, will you give me the pleasure of your company for a drive this afternoon, at, say, four o'clock?"

"I have not meant to be mysterious," she murmured. "If any inconsistency in my manner toward you has disturbed you, it is for me to ask your pardon. I will be most pleased to drive with you as you suggest."

Henry played the organ and sang for her. *Just a Song at Twilight*. Then they went into his adjoining office to discuss a possible position for her. She found herself coyly lowering her eyelids before the kindly, intense eyes of her new friend. And then the floor dropped beneath her feet and she fell into a dark shaft. Before she had time to shriek, all was rushing darkness, her skirt flew up, ballooning. How many feet per second does a body fall?

Henry made his way down to the secret cellar. He penetrated her still warm corpse and then dissected her, humming *Just a Song at Twilight*. He sold her skeleton to a medical student from the University of Illinois. Sometimes, pressed by other ventures—bigamy, insurance fraud—he had no time for his beloved dissection and merely cremated his victims in the furnace.

He had very few friends. One of the closest was Ben Pitezel, an alcoholic with a history of violence and a large family. Holmes became the family's benefactor. Long-suffering Carrie Pitezel and the children came to look on him as a kindly uncle.

Pitezel carried out various tasks for Holmes. He constructed long narrow boxes to hold articulated skeletons which Henry sold to medical colleges. Pitezel, posing as a butcher, sold barrels of fatty tissue labeled *Animal Fat* to a soap manufacturer.

THE CULTIVATED MIND OF HENRY HOLMES. TASTE IN MUSIC AND LITERATURE

Holmes loved to sing. He loved to read. He had a small, but interesting library: *Little Lord Fauntleroy, Ragged Dick, or Street Life in New York, Anarchy and Anarchists: A History of the Red Terror and the Social Revolution in America and Europe. Communism, Socialism and Nihilism in Doctrine and in Deed. The Chicago Haymarket Conspiracy and the Detention and Trial of the Conspirators. Hands Up! In the world of Crime. Twelve Years a Detective on the Chicago Police Force. 17,000 Arrests, 125 Penitentiary Convictions, 75 Young Girls Rescued From Lives of Shame* by C.R. Wooldridge.

Holmes committed to memory and could recite poems. There was "Asleep at the Switch"—"Think of the souls in the coming train and the graves you're sending them to. . ." There was "The Forced Bridal"—"Upon her cold and pallid brow. . ."

"A drunkard reached his cheerless home," he said softly to the empty drawing room, a generous tear in his eye. "The storm without was dark and wild. . ."

Another of Holmes's books was *The Scourge of Romanism* written by a priest who had fled from the Roman Catholic Church. The book revealed the sinister international conspiracy which emanated from the Vatican. The former priest was hounded by secret agents (mainly Irish thugs) who made attempts on his life. There were photos of actual correspondence between bishops and their minions.

There was also a photograph of a Catholic High School principal with a girl student on his knee. She wore a straw boater and flaunted a wine bottle. The principal's chair was placed in a forest. There were many trees in the background.

The book revealed that confessionals were equipped with trapdoors through which young women who admitted to carnal desires or acts were dropped into secret chambers where they became the objects of the priest's lust. This was where Henry got the idea for his own trapdoors.

The Great Babel Of Enjoyment

Chicago was changing at an amazing rate. The 1893 World's Fair was to be held there. The city braced itself for millions of visitors. Henry Holmes was ready for them too.

Chicago was two cities. The site of the Fair was the "White City." Augustus St. Gaudens called the Palace of Fine Art the greatest achievement since the Parthenon. There were statues by Loredo Taft, and Daniel Chester French. Frederic MacMonnies's fountain symbolized the Fair: Winged Fame stood at the prow of a vessel, Father Time used his scythe as a tiller, maidens swooned gracefully at the oars, cupids supported a pedestal where the goddess Columbia sat. Seahorses pranced. French's statue, *Republic*, was sixty-five feet tall. It looked solemn.

Meanwhile in the other Chicago, workers prepared for the Pullman Strike, racketeers walked the streets with panders, grafters, grifters, white slavers, burglars, pickpockets, blackmailers, boosters, safe-crackers, gamblers and yeggs. Cops on the beat were on the take. Kept aldermen and bought judges watched benignly. No seahorses pranced.

There was the Levee, a long row of bawdy houses and saloons which were frequented by women of all degrees of depravity. Some were consumptive, weak, thin and undernourished. Some had been compelled into the streets by swells who lived off them, leading lives of dress and ease, gambling, visiting the race track and fine theatres.

The women went from place to place, singing, yelling coarse jests. Everywhere there were desperate encounters. Young girls were enticed into Chinese laundries and given candy. Then they were induced to a whiff of an opium pipe. Detectives patrolled the Levee disguised as cattlemen. One played the dude, wearing a silk hat, red gloves, eye glasses, carrying a cane.

Enraged by gambling losses, crazed by drink, a young man attempted murder. Young girls from the country were enticed into lives of sin. Children were assaulted by ruffians.

SOLITARY PLEASURES

And meanwhile there was Henry Holmes's private world. He liked to walk alone in the park near his building. He liked the fountains, which were not in operation but free of debris in their dry basins. The grass was trimmed neatly. The gravel paths were free of litter and fallen leaves. Henry walked with an excited feeling of being alone in the world. He might be the last living being on earth. It was an odd feeling of displacement and an equally odd serenity. Let it come, he said inwardly, whatever it might be.

TWO WAIFS UPON THE TEMPEST

Minnie Williams and her sister Nannie came to the Fair. Kindly Harry Gordon, Minnie's fiance, met them at the train station. Minnie would never learn that Harry was actually Henry Holmes. Only one uncle and two older brothers stood between Minnie and a fortune. Holmes had already murdered the uncle in Forth Worth, Texas. Pitezel had done away with one of the brothers and Henry arranged for an industrial accident to befall the other brother.

Nannie was on one arm and Minnie on the other. Such a gallant escort. They heart Scott Joplin play a new kind of music. They saw a twenty-two thousand pound cheddar cheese from Ontario. They saw a fifteen hundred pound Venus de Milo made of chocolate. They ate ostrich egg omelettes, saw a model of the

Eiffel Tower and rode on George Ferris's immense new wheel. Then Henry took them back to his building where he fed them poisoned chocolates and so long at the fair.

FATAL TRAIN JOURNEYS

In one of Holmes's life insurance schemes Ben Pitezel was burned to death. An insurance investigator was suspicious. Holmes took Pitezel's children off on a train trip, soothing their mother with a story about going to meet Pitezel who was not dead.

He put Nellie and Alice Pitezel into a trunk in a house he had rented in Toronto and inserted a rubber tube into a hole in the trunk. The other end of the tube went to the gas jet. He buried them in the basement. Their brother Howard was buried in the cellar of a house in Irvington, Indiana. So many train rides.

THE AGE OF RAGGED DICK

This was the age of Carnegie, Gould, Fisk. Edison the boy hawked papers on the Michigan railroads. Then Edison the man became the wealthy inventor. James A. Farrel went from a menial job in a wire mill to become President of the United States Steel Corporation. Anything was possible. Henry Holmes was a clever man. He could have become anything. He chose to be what he was. It was a completely free choice.

OTHER FAMOUS CRIMINALS

The world since the death of Henry Holmes: Many criminals have come and gone. There was the Wild Bunch. Most of them died circa 1902—1912. The last of the gang, Walt Puntney, died in 1950. We've had Dillinger and Richard Speck. There was the fellow who got on top of that tower in Texas with a few rifles. Somebody else in that fast food restaurant. Bombs in airplanes, razor blades in apples, arsenic in medicine bottles, bombs in parked cars.

Smaller stuff: A child is crushed in a department store revolving door by somebody in a big hurry. A bus driver drags a passenger caught in the rear door to death despite the cries of the other passengers. A baby is born in a toilet a few blocks from the corner where Holmes's building stood. The baby's mother is a thirteen year old addict and prostitute. The baby's father may be that girl's father. Horror is everywhere we look. No big deal. There have been some wars. The term *serial killer* is coined.

I begin now to suspect that my fascination with Holmes is due to envy. Do I want to be him, to walk down the Nineties streets in my Prince Albert coat, my eyes keen above my moustache? Ah, the shy demure look in the corner of that girl's eye as she lifts her skirt stepping off the curb.

HEIR TO THE FIRES OF LUST

My house would have secret passages and tunnels. Rooms would be peepholed. Sliding panels would operate by invisible springs. The door bolts would be workable from the outside, a small hole bored into the lock's bolt. The hinges of the doors would be well greased and noiseless. Gas jets would be installed in some rooms. And the trap doors. Yes. I would glide down my corridors of pain like the ghost of Holmes.

Unlike Henry James, Henry Holmes never feared his own existence. He knew exactly who he was. Is this what I envy? Now I want to ride on the big Ferris Wheel and take in the Fair. Holmes's hand breaks through the cement and rises through the earth. It rises into sunlit air. I bend to take it in mine.

ORDINARY TIME

It was one of those rare summer days in Windsor when the humidity is low, the temperature moderate. It was a day of startling and clear blue. You can see the leaves on the trees in sculptured detail. You think every blade of grass could be counted. It is a poignant day, a delicate moment because as we who have lived here know, the usual is sure to come soon.

There will be dense dank humidity, fierce thunderstorms, tornado watches, tornado warnings and even the odd tornado. After unrelenting days of storm, the air is turgid, we move in effort through the damp hours and the trees hang down breathless.

But on these rare days when the summer sun seems beneficent and the breeze is just stiff enough to keep the sailboats on Lake St. Clair moving and keep the bugs away, the blue sky breaks your heart. The sun was dappling the long summer lawn through the trees. I thought *summer afternoon* to myself. The words are murmuring and elegaic.

On that particular day the women looked in perfect trim, like cemetery grass, pampered and worried over. They wore jewelry carelessly, as if there were lots more of it in the safety deposit box. The men wore forceful clothes. They knew who they were and what they were doing.

The light was lustrous, slanting, and gave a silvery sheen to everyone in it. The woman at the microphone was a forty-eight year old successful suburban woman who had a successful model agency and a successful marriage. Great. She had two daughters. One was in England studying design and the other had just graduated from the University of Florida. The woman liked horses and dogs and liked going to primo parties. She and her husband made a practice of never seeing the same people twice socially. It would be too boring. She disliked boredom and red meat. Since her children grew up she and her husband have rediscovered romance. She goes to private dancing classes.

I know all this about her because she was profiled in today's paper. Why do I dislike her? She is at the microphone to tell us why we are all here. We are present to support a worthy cause. We are protesting the unjust imprisonment of a great South American poet.

Well. It isn't exactly imprisonment in the way we imagine it—electrodes attached to genitals and so on. He is under house arrest and forbidden to speak publicly or to write anything.

We had heard a professor from the University's Spanish Department read some of the poet's work. And now the chairperson (she of the primo parties) was telling us how our funds would be effectively channelled and coordinated with initiatives in other venues. (Those are the words she used.)

"Excuse me," said a woman seated at the next table, "Think I know you."

She was about the same age as our chairperson and by her insouciant clothing I judged that she was of the same social class. Yet I surmised also that she was a nicer person.

"I'm visiting," I said. "Staying with the Goodes. I used to teach with Asa."

"You're not from Windsor?" she smiled.

She was attractive, but I am usually over-influenced by others showing interest in me. My judgement tends to be untrustworthy.

"No," I said, turning my chair towards here. "My wife was. She was born here."

"Maybe I know her," she said.

A waiter with swift panache poured more wine into our glasses.

"I doubt it," I said. "She moved when she was very young. Grew up in California."

"Is she here?"

"She's dead."

"Oh."

"A little over a year ago," I said. "It was her own choice."

The umbrella tables reminded me of one I sat at in the South of France. The umbrellas shake in the breeze. In late afternoon, people hurry past with their baguettes. The evening meal is important to the French. There is seriousness in the manner of the people with their groceries going home. Others in beach thongs and swimming suits are looking at postcard racks. They are obviously tourists and indifferent to serious dining.

"I *did* live here for a while," I said. "Back in the late Sixties. Couple of years. Funny. Lived in the same neighbourhood my wife had. We discovered this later on."

I was remembering the smell of the original Lifebuoy soap. The colour of it was coral, like the inside of a conch. Nothing in the world today comes close to that clean smell. It had been the smell of summer, of white trousers and walking on an old dock and sailboats creaking and bobbing in their slips.

I was just drunk enough to feel maudlin. I was thinking that our chairperson wasn't so bad after all. And the woman I was chatting up hadn't mentioned a husband yet. Usually they do that soon in the conversation.

I used to believe in literature. I mean that I didn't just read the books. I believed them. But now as I think back it seems that what they told me was that people keep on making the same mistakes over and over and over. How did I miss that essential message?

The books told me that people are kind and foolish and thoughtless and careless. They can be capable of great cruelty and awesome pettiness. They sacrificed their lives for dumb ideals and for a bit of fluff or a twitch of a skirt throw away a lifetime's work.

But sometimes they can be generous and thoughtful and kind. When you try to add it all up it simply does not make sense.

Now when I think back to insignificant times—at least they seemed unimportant back then— they take on extraordinary meaning. Like the way a light fell on a corner of an ordinary street on an ordinary day. Now that oblique light seems to transcend itself. Those moments of over-reaching plenitude—

By now the woman and I were side by side at her table. Her name was Mary Beth and she was a Systems Analyst. I told her that I was no longer teaching and that I was in the Private Sector. She was divorced. Children grown. I told her I had no children.

My father is a no longer valid passport in a drawer in my bedroom. Sometimes I look at it. The face in the passport photo is trying not to smile, attempting to be serious, trying to convince potential border authorities that the bearer is a good citizen. Will be willing to respect the laws and customs of the country. Once a respected tourist, now my father was a shade among shadows.

My mother is still alive in a rest home in Illinois. My father used to read the Sunday comics to me. Using many dramatic voices. There was a single-panel cartoon called *Out Our Way* and another called *Major Hoople's Boarding House*. Even as long ago as it was when my father read to me, the world in those comics seemed already old and lost. Imagine a world where there were boarding houses, lorded over by massive matriarchs. Can a matriarch do an actual lording?

The meals were communal and the matriarch's spouse was a layabout spinner of tall tales. He wore a Turkish smoking cap and slippers in the evening when the only entertainment was the communal newspaper in the parlour and listening to the Major's lies.

Perhaps the boarders worked in the shops depicted in *Out Our Way*. It was a world of working men who inhabited the mills and shops and who were not sullen, uppity or upwardly mobile. Life was wholistic. Children were pesky by nature and therefore either to be punished or ignored. It was a pre-Freudian world where masculine companionship was prized over heterosexual activities which led inexorably to marriage, nagging and responsibilities (i.e. the pesky children.)

For women it was obviously the same trap from another perspective. Yet there was no sense of revolt in these panels, first intoned by my father and later read by myself alone. The world was accepted. It was America before Freud and the union movement. It was a world of screen doors slamming in the summer and men with lunch pails and boys in caps and no air conditioners. It was also a world of no pain, no war, no illness and no death.

I think I was trying to explain all this to Mary Beth.

The speeches were long over and the sun was slanting at an unbearable angle. Soon it would be full evening. I kept on trying to explain my lost world. Mary Beth looked sympathetic. But of course she had been keeping up with me, glass of wine for glass.

"I guess it's natural for us to want the good thing to go on," I said. "It's like listening to Wagner or—all that unfulfilled and aching desire held in tension. That tip-toe effect in Keats. Keep things from resolution by force of will. Cold pastoral. Not cold in the sense of being the opposite of warmth—"

"I'll be right back," Mary Beth said, laying a firm hand on my forearm. "Just a little trip to the powder room."

A state of no-temperature, I thought staring at the umbrella above me swaying gently in the evening breeze. Nonhuman because it is so deep in the human.

"Comes out only in dreams." I said aloud. "In waking daylight we are simply not gods in an arcadian forest."

"I beg your pardon?" said a woman across the table from me.

"We move in ordinary time," I said. "I think I better go check on Mary Beth. I think she has been gone a very long time."

The grass was unsteady beneath my feet. People were starting to leave. The waiters were doing closing-up things at the portable bar. Inside the sun room there were two Eighteenth Century engravings framed and flanking the door to the rest of the house where presumably there was a powder room and Mary Beth. One engraving depicted a woman wearing a Grecian style gown seated on an ornate chair. She was reading a parchment held up to her by two cherubs. A bearded and dejected old man was kneeling at the side of her chair, his wrists bound behind his back. Between two pillars a full-sailed ship was leaving port. Obviously this was an allegory of the countess of something subduing Time and sponsoring an enterprise. The other engraving was a ho-hum Arch of Titus.

I went in between the engravings. People were doing serious drinking. Someone gave me a scotch on the rocks in a real glass. I was introduced to the chairperson whose name was Heidi. Up close she exuded a hoydenish quality. I started to temper my original impression. She gave me a crinkly-eyed smile. Someone said that she had been the Celeb of the Day in the paper. Yes, I said, I saw that.

Mary Beth found me. She suggested that we go for some food. She said one of the best Chinese restaurants in North America was in Windsor.

On the way there she mentioned that the restaurant was close to her home. This fact held great portent in my muddled imagination. After she said it, the fact lay between us on the seat in her air conditioned Aries, silent and uneasy.

I have been very lonely since Debbie died. Debbie is not a serious name. But her final act was very serious. My going to the South of France was a mistake. The place was full of memories. I should have gone someplace where we had never been together.

Debbie, like Heidi, had rediscovered romance. When it didn't work out, she did something even more romantic. That is what I mean by a literary situation: what the books told me about the fragility and perversity of human nature.

The Chinese food may have been good. I remember throwing it up in the bushes in Mary Beth's yard. She put on a cassette of some baroque composer. The music was deeply serious, urgent, often at times vigorous and playful. It was never, however, frivolous. It held its dignity like a man waltzing at his granddaughter's wedding.

"The erosions that language has gone through," I said afterwards. "Formidable."

I had difficulty with the word. Mary Beth made small noises of agreement .

"Now we're all so subtle and cunning. Only the faint echo of what's been left out. All our frontal lobe stuff keeps us from the simple, real thing—"

I think I must have said more. I woke up to sunlight coming in the blinds. I was in bed and Mary Beth's hair was all over my pillow. I woke up suddenly, feeling dry-mouthed shock and shame. In my confusion of feelings somehow uppermost was inordinate guilt over my violation of the hospitality of the Goodes.

Mary Beth was obviously a morning person. She woke up easily, smiled generously and gave me a proprietary embrace. I am not a man for dalliance. Since Debbie's death I have not "dated" or gone to the haunts of the single. For one thing I presume that I am past the upper limit of age range for eligible singles. For another I fear that I am something of a pedantic bore. Right at that moment, I was feeling (besides the guilt of the Bad Guest) that I had committed boredom on Mary Beth.

However, her continuing cheerfulness would seem to say otherwise. While she hummed and bustled in the kitchen I shuddered in the bathroom, avoiding the accusing mirror and used toothpaste on my finger.

Dressed in yesterday's clothes, I mourned over the coffee in the overbright kitchen. Then I refused a ride, pleaded the need to return to the Goodes and left, after we kissed a tender goodbye and I promised to call later on.

As I walked down the street I realized that I was in my old neighbourhood. There was the apartment building I had lived in. There was the street where Debbie spent her childhood. Synchronistic. I was beginning to feel like a human being again, coming alive inside yesterday's clothes, walking down yesterday's street.

Asa and Emmie were cool and full of unexpressed reproach. I left on the afternoon train. I stared out the window at the ripe fields.

Now, sometime later, the Goodes have forgiven me. The famous poet was suddenly allowed to leave his house and country. He came to New York to attend an international writer's congress. He was enthusiastically listened to and given much respect. I shall never know how much our money and efforts did to effect this surprising release.

But when I told Asa that Mary Beth and I were to be married, he said something about "settling for less." He had always admired Debbie to excess. I remember being jealous. In any case, I did not feel as if I were settling for less. Mary Beth and I discussed places where we might honeymoon. She suggested the South of France.

I said it was too hot in August. She mentioned her son and wife and grandson in Ottawa. I said it was hot and humid there too. We went to Illinois and combined our nuptial trip with a celebration of my mother's ninetieth birthday.

Often when I visit her she thinks I am my younger brother who was killed in Korea. Sometimes she thinks I am my father. Other times she does not know me at all. On this occasion she was lucid although she kept calling Mary Beth Debbie.

After our visit we went on into Wisconsin where neither of us had been before. We stopped at an Inn near the Wisconsin Dells. Aeons ago, glaciation tore away immense chunks of rock to form the high cliffs surrounding Devil's Lake. The ice also shaped the steep river gorges in the area. Guidebooks would call the Dells "picturesque." I bought a postcard showing a dog leaping from one tower-shaped rock to another. The photographer caught the dog in mid-leap, suspended high in the air. Presumably the dog made his leap successfully. I sent the postcard to the Goodes.

It is a good time to be here. It is late in the season and the Inn is not crowded. It seems less hectic than other places I've been. It ticks to a slower clock. I could almost imagine the smell of the old coral Lifebuoy soap on my skin after a shower, walking onto the screened-in porch at dinnertime, growing young inside my skin.

The Inn is old-fashioned, like an old boarding house where people always sit in the same place for meals and small pleasantries are exchanged. We do not become too forward or take liberties because, after all, our stay here is only temporary.

We have not rediscovered romance. What we have found is something less fevered and literary, but is all the more precious and worth keeping. It is ordinary, like the time after Pentecost. It is a sedate, stately and mild time.

Like people posing for passport photographs, Mary Beth and I walk out of the Inn after dinner, staring through the camera at the places we are going to. We move towards the dock. I imagine leaving a dark harbour for the open sea.

Is that a romantic fantasy? I hope not. I am an ordinary man holding his wife's hand as we walk towards the water in the evening light.

I long to be at one with the visible world. In Windsor and Toronto cars placidly go by on side streets, going home, each driver's face set and intent on his own journey, a negligent casual arm on the open car window's ledge, radios set on a chosen station. I want to be among them, going home to Mary Beth. She is watering the flowers on our apartment balcony. She looks down at the street, watches for our car. The afternoon sun slants lower.

Here, back at the Inn, we walk to the water's edge and stand for a while looking out hopefully at the setting sun.

NOTES TOWARDS A DESCRIPTIVE CATALOGUE OF IMMENSE PAINTINGS

The human imagination, faced with the concept of nothingness, absence and the cessation of existence, erects strategies in defense. Epic poems, story-telling, dramas. And paintings.

During the Nineteenth Century there was a vogue for big pictures. It was as if for a time artists thought that their creative powers were commensurate with the vastness of Nature. Not much survives of these grandiose attempts. Some were simply lost. Others were never finished.

Washington Allston's Unfinished Big Painting.

Benjamin Robert Haydon and The Dwarf.

Keats mentions dining with Haydon in the same letter that he defines *Negative Capability* and also speaks of Benjamin West's *Death On a Pale Horse*. Haydon lacked Negative .Capability and despised West.

Mr John Whiteway of Fishwick (on the Tergin) bought an immense Haydon painting and had to remove a large window in the drawing room in order to get it into the house. Large paintings are hard to handle, move around, hang and find enough wall space to begin with.

Washington Allston was one of the most popular American painters in the first half of the Nineteenth Century. He came back from a triumphant visit to England and the Continent in 1818. He had turned down the opportunity to paint one of the pictures in the Rotunda in the Capitol in Washington because he was finishing what he thought would be his greatest—and largest—painting: *Belshazzar's Feast*. He showed the all-but finished work to Gilbert Stuart who was impressed but thought the perspective all wrong. He suggested a shift in the point of view. Allston began to redo the painting. He spent over twenty years reworking it.

At seven in the evening of July 9, 1843, Allston, having dined with his family, went back to his studio to work on *Belshazzar*. He had to climb a ladder to get to the soothsayer's face. He had to descend to get a proper perspective on his progress. Then back up again, down the ladder again. Tiresome work.

He re-entered the house from his studio and spoke to his niece, Miss Charlotte Dana. His words—to be among his last—counselled intellectual, moral and religious development. He closed with a chaste kiss on her forehead, saying "God bless you, my child."

Afterwards he complained to his wife of a slight indigestion. Whilst she prepared a dose of soda, he sat in front of the fire, his head resting on his hand as if in thought, perhaps about the work that remained to be done on his giant painting. His wife spoke to him. He did not reply. She touched his hand. It was limp. Her sister and niece ran to her assistance. They laid him out on the rug in front of the fireplace and chafed his body. A doctor had been summoned. He came in, his face solemn. He took Allston's pulse, sighed and shook his head. "He is gone," the doctor said in a hushed tone.

Allston was buried in Cambridge. Harvard students bearing torches led the cortege into the graveyard. Overshadowing night clouds opened and the body of Allston was bourne to the grave in starlight.

Belshazzar's Feast covers twelve by sixteen feet of canvas. The seated King had been finished but was, *in pentimento*, covered over with a coat of dark brown paint. Like a shroud. The prophet, Daniel, eyes fixed terribly on the King, raises his hand to point to the writing on the wall. Chaldean astrologers stand to Daniel's right. A little back from the foreground is a group of devout Jews. One of them kneels in reverence. Another tries to touch the garment of the prophet. A banqueting table is laden with rich opulence. Large columns of porphyry support a gallery filled with awestruck spectators.

Different areas of the painting had been pumiced down. The heads of many figures were unfinished. The skin colouring was dead. The heads seemed larger, out of proportion to the figures.

Some chalk outlines:

1. An outline around the toes of the King's left foot. It was obviously to be lengthened.

2. A depression around the heel of Daniel's left foot. Something to do with the new point of view.

3. In the upper left corner, a green curtain hanging down, covering one of the pillars, had been pumiced down. The chalk lines extended to a golden candlestick.

Could one say that the unfinished picture is a monument to Allston's inner growth in creative imagination? His skill and physical powers could not keep pace with the accelerated state of his mental and moral faculties?

Allston knew Coleridge. He knew of Haydon's work through Coleridge. When he finally saw *Christ's Entry Into Jerusalem* he came out of the exhibit, his face lit with pure delight. A critic asked him, "Is there not there this and that defect?"

"O yes," Allston said. "But the picture has genius and life. It has glorious parts and one need not see its defects."

Wordsworth knew of Allston through Coleridge's reports of him.

"By the reports of his conversation and corresponding accounts of his noble qualities of heart and temper," Wordsworth said, "I was led to admire, and with truth I May say, to love Mr. Allston, before I had seen him or his works."

Once Allston and Coleridge travelled in Italy. They stopped at a decrepit inn. Allston, bored, took up a book lying about which turned out to be the veriest lubricious trash. Coleridge came in and glancing over Allston's shoulder, said "You may be amused. But you had better be doing nothing. You cannot touch pitch without being defiled."

"How vast, how dread, o'erwhelming is the thought
Of space interminable!"

Allston wrote those words in a sonnet on Michelangelo.

Allston's large painting *The Angel Releasing St. Peter* is in the chapel of the Hospital For the Insane in Worcester, Mass.

The essayist William Hazlitt once asked Allston where he found the models for his heads as he had never seen any like them in London. In fact, Hazlitt went on, some of them looked rather Asiatic. Allston said that he didn't paint from models. He made them up out of his own imagination. Hazlitt looked incredulous. He called Allston a liar.

There were other big paintings. In 1801 the bones of a "carnivorous animal of immense size" were found in New York State. Charles Willson Peale paid a small army of workers to dig. He painted a record of the find: *Exhuming the Mastodon* which he hung in his own museum. Actually there were two skeletons, when sorted out. One was put together and set up in the museum and the other was sent to London.

Thomas Cole also wrestled with a big painting, left unfinished at his death. *The Cross and the World* was full of murky religious symbolism. Other big paintings by Cole include *The Course of Empire* and *The Voyage of Life*.

The big painting *Christ's Entry Into Jerusalem* in Charles Willson Peale's museum is not by Haydon. It is by Henry Sargent. He lived in Boston.

No relation to John Singer Sargent who made a good living doing regular-sized portraits of society ladies and hobnobbed with Henry James. Sometimes, smaller is better.

Benjamin Robert Haydon would learn that smaller was sometimes more popular. To his sorrow.

Christ's Triumphant Entry Into Jerusalem.

Benjamin Robert Haydon had a Napoleonic conception of himself. He often compared his career with Napoleon's. He spoke often of his genius and attempted immense works of art. In 1820 he exhibited the nineteen by sixteen foot picture of Christ entering Jerusalem in the Egyptian Hall in London. He had taken six years to finish the work. He did the head of Christ six times, trying to combine power and humility. Power ultimately won. It took three men to carry the painting from his studio to the Hall where it was framed. The frame weighed six hundred pounds. In front of the somewhat arrogant Savior, the Samaritan woman and a penitent girl spread their garments. There was the centurian and there was a mocking Voltaire, a head bowed Wordsworth, Isaac Newton and Keats, all in the crowd.

Eight hundred invitations had been sent out for the private opening. Foreign ambassadors, society beauties, bishops and members of the literati came. Mrs. Sarah Siddons proclaimed that the figure of Christ was "completely successful." The Persian ambassador admired an elbow. The public opening,later, was equally successful.

It was a different story in 1846 when Haydon planned to exhibit his latest big pictures—*Aristides Being Hooted by the Multitude* and *Nero Harping While Rome Burned*. P.T. Barnum was in town with his midget Tom Thumb, also booked in the Egyptian Hall. In the first week, Tom Thumb was seen by twelve thousand gawkers and only three hundred people came to see Haydon's new work. Haydon had forebodings before the opening. He took his wife to the station to go down to Brighton. On the way the horse fell down. So did one of the paintings on the morning of the private show. Haydon went to work on his next opus, *King Alfred and the First English Jury*. It would never be finished. In June, 1846, Haydon wrote down the "Last Thoughts of B.R. Haydon." As usual, Napoleon was in his mind. So was Tom Thumb. Haydon put a pistol to his head. A bad shot. Grasping a razor, he hacked at his throat. He succeeded, splashing blood on King Alfred. Tom Thumb finished his final week at the Egyptian Hall, singing two songs: *Farewell to Albion* and *Then You'll Remember Me.*

George Cruikshank did two etchings of Haydon and Tom Thumb. One showed a despondent painter ,the other a dwarf lounging in luxury. "Born a Genius" and "Born a Dwarf."

In that same year John Banvard exhibited his *Panorama of the Mississippi* in Boston.

Banvard's Panorama of the Mississippi Painted on Three Miles of Canvas Exhibiting a View of Country Twelve Hundred Miles in Length.

It was painted on three miles of canvas, stored on giant spools. The spools unwound, the painting moved. Banvard lectured as it unwound, recited poems, told jokes. A pianoforte played. The panorama was a great success. Congress passed special resolutions praising Banvard for his "boldness, originality and indefatigable perseverance." Banvard took the panorama to England. His Command Performance in St Georges Hall, Windsor was a sellout. Some big paintings are successful, others not. In 1848 John Rowson Smith did a *four* mile panorama of the Mississippi. It too had its moment. Banvard's painting was ultimately cut into panels and sold to theatres to be used as stage curtains. Some of the theatres became nickelodeons and then movie theatres and then, in time, were torn down. Some of these theatres were in: Columbia, Missouri; Macomb, Illinois; Berwyn, Illinois; Evansville, Indiana and River Falls, Wisconsin. Nobody knows what has happened to the Banvard canvases.

Other theatres reputed to have part of the Banvard panorama: Pullman, Washington and La Grande, Oregon. The theatre in Berwyn, Illinois was the Ritz.

Description of the curtain in the Ritz Theatre, Berwyn, Illinois: A levee with a steamboat departing. Sweat-shiny black men stripped to the waist are rolling barrels up a plank towards a wagon. Two women stand off to the right, looking at the steamboat. Their faces are hidden by the parasols they are carrying. Twin trails of smoke from the steamboat traverse the sky.

In the same year that *Christ's Entry Into Jerusalem* was successfully exhibited, Rembrandt Peale unveiled his own big painting in Baltimore. *The Court of Death* showed a young man struck down at the feet of Death. Old Age was supported by Virtue. There were the figures of Want, Desolation, Dread, Gout, Dropsy, Hypochondria and Intemperance. Peale's allegory was plain: death was brought on by man's own foibles—ignorance and impulses towards self-destruction. The painting was a sensation wherever it was exhibited. In Albany, New York a senator dropped dead as he entered the exhibition hall. This added to the frisson. Over thirty thousand people paid a total of nine thousand dollars to see it. Over one hundred thousand colored engravings of it were sold at a dollar each.

Haydon's wife was going down to Brighton. Her nerves would not stand the strain of the exhibit, the crowds, the last frantic minutes. On the morning of the opening they set out for Victoria Station. The streets were still wet from the night rain. The cab horse's hooves slid on the uneven cobbles and the horse went down. The cab's shaft cracked like a pistol shot. There was a hullabaloo of cabmen and shouting costermongers. Haydon remembered that the same thing had happened to Napoleon just before Waterloo. Haydon sat in the unmoving cab feeling the dread of omen creep up from his feet.

Haydon hated Tom Thumb. He hated his little fingers and his tiny feet. There was something in the miniature that Haydon feared. He dreamed small dreams and saw himself shrinking in an inexorable slide towards nothing.

Haydon had always been convinced of his own genius. In 1804 when he first arrived in London he was just eighteen. He knelt and prayed to God to make him a great painter. He would revive historical painting, found a national school and raise the low level of English art. He found patrons. Wordsworth addressed a sonnet to him.

He was plagued by poor eyesight. When painting he wore thick eyeglasses. His method was to see his model and picture from a great distance, and then to take off the glasses and go to the canvas. Then on with the glasses and stepping far back. Then he would examine the result, using a mirror and two pair of eyeglasses. The method sometimes resulted in grotesque disproportion. Many of his heroic figures had absurdly short legs. He noted this sometimes but did not bother to correct. He was too convinced of his own genius.

He espoused good causes: schools of design, government sponsored frescoes in public buildings, monuments (government commissioned) to public figures. His own abrasive personality did these causes more harm than good.

The sound of a church bell, solemn, hollow, round. Iron reverberating.

There was no answering in Haydon. A chill hung in the air. He stared at the catastrophe ahead of him, the horse struggling to gain purchase on the wet cobbles, the men shouting. Haydon knew that the Queen had received a visit from the dwarf and had given him a gift. She lived in the past. No modern queen had a personal dwarf. It was an unfashionable desire, harking back to less democrat times. Now this Yankee midget. Haydon gritted his teeth as he imagined Tom Thumb strutting in the palace, the petted darling of the Royal children. Haydon felt the sting of injured merit.

He was about to be separated from his beloved wife. However, life must have been anxious for her. They slept in separate bedrooms for about a year after each new baby arrived. They arrived every eighteen months or so. At table, his behaviour was erratic. His head was crowded with visions of ancient heroes, of Biblical spectacles, principles of ancient art, humourous subjects, deductions, sarcastic attacks on the Academy, pictures of his beloved children—

"I paint," he wrote. "I converse, write and fall asleep, start up refreshed, eat my lunch with the fierceness of a Polyphemus, walk, dine, read the paper, return to my study to contemplate what I have been doing, or muse until dusk, then to bed lamenting my mortality at being fatigued. I never rest. I talk all night in my sleep, start up—I scarce know whether I shall relish ruin—

The head of Christ had given him a lot of trouble. Dark eyes and a fierce brow made the Savior look too human, too given to passions. Haydon did it over at least six times. It became in turn bland, too pure, too serene, sublime, compassionate, insipid. Mrs. Siddons, however, found it *supernatural.*

Nobody bought it. The show was a great success for Haydon's creditors. Haydon moved the painting to Edinburgh and Glasgow. It was a success. Nobody bought it. A critic said of the donkey in the painting that it was almost worthy to rank with that in Tintoretto's *Flight Into Egypt.* Keats, Wordsworth and Elizabeth Bartlett wrote poems about him. In 1808 he saw the Elgin Marbles in shabby circumstances—in a dank shed behind Lord Elgin's Park Lane house. Haydon felt the future. He was set on fire. It seemed to him that a divine truth blazed inside of him. He planned big subjects:

Milton Playing on His Organ
Adam Reconciling Eve After Her Dream
Samson Pulling Down the Philistines
A Woman Contemplating the Body of a Man She Has Just Murdered
The Spirit of Caesar Appearing to Brutus
A Mother Dashing Down a Precipice With Her Child
A Scene in a Madhouse

None of these were attempted.
Now, the memory of his big success when Mrs. Siddons announced it and the Persian ambassador admired a soldier's arm rankled and festered. "Awoke at three," he wrote. "In very

great agony of mind and lay awake till long after five. . .There lay Aristides and Nero, unasked for, unfelt for, rolled up. . ."

"I sat from two till five," he wrote later, "Staring at my picture like an idiot. My brain pressed down by anxiety and thoughts of my dear Mary and children. . .I dined, after having raised money on our silver. . ."

He kept the shutters half closed in his studio. He preferred to work in semidarkness. A cupboard with volumes of poetry in different languages hung over a writing table. An open Bible lay on the table. Passages of special consolation had markers set in so that they could be turned to quickly. From Edgware Road came the sound of wheels and horse's hooves.

It had been very warm for days. He was despondent over his debts, the disdain of the Academy and the indignity of Tom Thumb's public success. He dined with a friend at Hampstead. Flushed and haggard, he spoke of suicide.

He bought a pair of pistols at a gun maker's shop in Oxford Street. At 10:45 his wife and daughter heard a shot. They supposed it to be caused by troops mustering in the Park. Five minutes later there was a heavy thud in the studio. They supposed it was one of the big canvases being moved. Mrs Haydon left for Brixton. Her daughter went a little way with her and then returned to see if she could console her father.

The door to the studio was not locked. In the dim light the room seemed empty. Her father's watch lay next to the Bible, ticking loudly. Then she saw him lying at the base of the painting. Thinking he had thrown himself down to study the foreground of the painting, she went up to him and bent to touch his shoulder. She slipped in what she thought was paint. She was standing in her father's blood.

The next day a great thunderstorm all over England broke the fierce heat.

On his tombstone: *He devoted 42 years to the improvement of the Taste of the English People in high art and died brokenhearted from pecuniary distress.*

Keats knew another side of Haydon: vanity, grandiloquence, a tendency to swanning about and the cold habit of borrowing and not paying back money.

An early work, *The Judgment of Solomon* was twelve by ten feet. Tom Taylor edited Haydon's *Autobiography*. Taylor was also the author of a play, *Our American Cousin*. Lincoln was watching this play when he was assassinated.

Haydon on the Elgin Marbles:

"I sketched the marbles ten, fourteen and fifteen hours at a time; staying often till twelve at night holding a candle and my board in one hand and drawing with the other. . .I have drank my tea at one in the morning . .and looked at my picture and dwelt on my drawings, and pondered on the change of empires and thought that I had been contemplating what Socrates looked at and Plato saw. . ."

So there we have it. The vogue for big pictures has passed. There are three figures lying before them: Allston falling before his fire. Haydon self-immolated before his last, unfinished big painting. A New York state senator in the midst of Peale's exhibit. As if all were struck down by the over-reaching. The Greeks had a word for it.

This is an age for dwarfs.

THE DARK SUMMER

Two rabbis discussed and disputed as they walked along a country road. Suddenly there was someone else with them, joining in the debate. Then the third person vanished as suddenly as he had appeared.

The Colony was awash with talent.There were drama students, visual artists, composers, photographers, video artists and the inevitable dancers in residence. Alan was the only writer in the Colony that summer. He was a bit older than most of the other residents. He felt the air charged with ego. Drama students made entrances and exits. Sometimes they made an exeunt, severally. Their faces were eager, expressive, over-expressive. The dancers moved as if hovering an inch or so off the common earth with their little bun heads and their little buns.

Alan felt a mingle of feelings about his fellow colonists. There was so much damned youth and talent and determination. And they were so damned boorish. The dancers were the worst, cutting in the cafeteria line without apology. Once he was getting orange juice from a machine and a little dancer enjambed herself under his arm to get at the grapefruit juice spigot. Such self-centered egotism was awesome. Alan felt admiration, pity and distaste.

The William Surrey Halleck Colony for the Arts is near the Sangre de Cristo Mountains north of Santa Fe. The San Juan Mountains and the Rio Chama River are to the west of the Colony.

Edith Woodrow Halleck founded and endowed the Colony in 1906, two years after her husband, William, died of consumption. William had been a composer. Ill most of his life, he had not composed much. Edith had been studying painting in Boston when she met William. After their marriage she did not paint much. She devoted her life to caring for William. Money was no problem. Edith was the only child of Charles Haldan Woodrow, railroad baron.

Edith took William to the Southwest, hoping for succor from the salubrious climate. After William died in Santa Fe, Edith decided to found a colony as a memorial to him. She ran the place until her death in 1927.

When Edith's workers broke ground, the nearest town was thirty miles to the south. As time passed, a little support community grew near the Colony, taking its name from it. Halleck now has a population of about three hundred, a post office, a gas station and a big log cabin style roadhouse where there is western music and dancing on the weekends. There is a footpath running downhill from the Colony into town. The path passes a small cemetery with a prominent mausoleum in the center of it. William and Edith's.

Alan's studio was in the woods behind the residence. The way to the studio lay between music practice huts. From one came the sound of a violin plucked, plucked. He glanced in the window. A young girl bent to her instrument. She looked oriental. She had not seen him looking in. From another hut came flute, from another, piano. The pianist was female, had short curly hair, thin semitic face. From further off came a cello. As he walked, the various musics impinged and his progress down the path made, he thought with pleasure, a kind of fantasia of his own.

A girl was coming down the path towards him. She had a pert chin and short hair. The chin was up, defiant, and her eyes brimmed with tears. He felt a Whitmanesque urge to enfold, comfort her. He did not, of course, do anything. The gesture would have been rebuffed, misunderstood, scorned and wasted. The girl passed him as if he were not there. His music fell behind him. He went on to his studio.

There was a patch of early morning sunlight on the carpet outside the dining room. He looked at it, his pen poised over the notebook. He wrote:

Two rabbis discussed and disputed as they walked down a country road. Suddenly there was someone else with them, joining in the discussion. Then the third person vanished—

A shadow fell across the light on the carpet. A woman appeared in the doorway. She had short curly hair and a thin clever face. Was it the pianist? She looked intently around the room, turned and went away. The patch of sunlight lay there.

How to describe the light here, he wrote. *A kind of washed light, rinsed and young and new. As if it were the first light. Hurts the eyes. A good hurting—*

The resident music director, Caspar something-something, came in. He had been born in Austria some seventy years ago. He sounded and looked like the late Bela Lugosi. Alan smiled and inclined his head. Caspar did not notice the gesture.

For the past three days it had rained incessantly. But now the sun lay sprawled on the carpet. Perhaps better days lay ahead. Alan closed his notebook. Time to get back to the studio. On his way out of the dining room he stopped to look at the large portrait of Edith Woodrow hanging near the door. It had been painted about 1916. Edith was posed wearing Indian clothing and a rug hung in back of her. Her hair was in braids. She had big naive eyes. She had a strong rather than a pretty face. Alan wondered what the local Indians had thought of her, dressing up and all.

There was an old story that the Colony had been built on sacred burial grounds. But other stories asserted that the Indians liked Edith, were grateful to her for all sorts of generosity.

Someone passed quickly behind him. He half turned. It was the thin-faced pianist.

"Hello," she said in a bright face, smiling.

She went into the dining room. Alan walked out of the building and down the path into his music.

James Blasco entered the dining room the next morning. He entered the room as if he were an opera impresario and expected everyone to know who he was. He looked like the portrait of Fauré by Sargent. He was, in fact, an opera impresario The opera currently in production at the Colony was based on the story of Harun ar Rashid, the caliph of Baghdad who put on beggar's rags and went into the streets to learn what his people's lives were really like.

The libretto included the kidnapping of a Princess, the entrance of banditti into a grotto, the march and chorus of the janissaries, and the rustic dance of maidens carrying baskets of fruit and flowers. Alan had gone to a few open rehearsals. He knew that the final act would include the denouncing of the Grand Vizier and the revelation of the caliph's true identity. There would be a duet with the caliph and the Princess.

Alan wondered how he could get out of attending the premiere. Colonists were expected to support one another. The opera, he thought, would be bearable. But there would be the afterglow party with Blasco hugging people, kissing cheeks, and swanning about. There would be curtsies and bunches of flowers. Squeals and bellows of self-congratulation. All that sort of swank.

And there was Blasco, in the dining room, large as life and twice as unnatural, approaching and then sitting with Caspar. Alan nodded to them as he left the room. They were intent in conversation and did not respond.

The support staff were all young, enthusiastic, athletic and tended to bustle a great deal. All wore pagers on their belts. The pagers beeped incessantly. The staff never got to finish a conversation. They were constantly rushing off to answer phone messages They were all cheerful and over-helpful. Alan had, sometimes, the odd feeling that he was in that television series *The Prisoner* with its "village" full of orderly, smiling, placid guests and guards. If he made a run for the mountains a big balloon would bounce and roll after him. The place was too good to be true. Yet Alan moved through his days as if invisible. He was in a crowd, yet alone.

Alan met the pianist with the thin face on the residence elevator one morning. Her name was Jessica. He ran into her again a day or so later at lunchtime. He was behind her in the line. She invited him to join her. Two of her friends were already at the table. Jackie and Jeanne. Three "J's." A frieze of young women. Jeanne was the girl with the pert chin he had seen on the path. She seemed over her sorrow.

Jessica with the thin face and curly hair was a pianist. Jackie was a sculptor. Jeanne was a video artist. Jackie looked impatient, ready to go even while she was sitting still. She got up for more coffee. Alan thought that her legs looked as if they wanted to play hopscotch. She was tall and her hair was dark and braided like Edith's. She had a kind of don't mess with me air mingled with shy flirting. Jeanne seemed happy to have met Alan. For the first time in weeks Alan felt in communion with his fellow human beings. He was reluctant to leave the table and start the day's work. How lovely they were, his frieze of young women.

One of the perks of the place was free admission to any of the artist's showcase recitals. He was scheduled to give a reading of his work in progress in the final week of the residency. He felt uneasy about it and was reassured by going to the showcases. Audiences were mainly supportive. One afternoon he went to a performance of Messiaen's *Quartet For the End of Time*. He had been working all day and was half-asleep. Then there was a slow movement, a kind of dialogue between a wistful cello and a sedate piano. A man, he thought, walks with his young daughter. She speaks shyly, swiftly. The man's head is bent to the side to listen as they step along. Her words, sweetly shy, his steps grave, dignified and tender. I have, Alan thought, no daughter.

He woke up the next morning early to ungodly shrieking. Kids, maybe the young dancers. He looked at the digital alarm. Six bloody AM. Too early for kid's pranks. Some kind of animal. Wolf or coyote. It sounded like a child in pain or joy.

"Say," he said later at breakfast. "Did anybody hear that awful racket? Some kind of animal?"

"I heard nothing," said Caspar.

Jackie said she had heard nothing. Jeanne wasn't sure. The third "J" was not at breakfast. Alan checked later with some of the staff. Nobody had heard the animal. It might have been a coyote someone said.

He went to Jessica's recital. It was Ravel. Jessica wore a dark dress and crystal earrings that glistened like small teardrops next to her ears. That proud profile. She played with restrained passion.

Alan remembered that someone once said to Ravel that she had been deeply moved by some piece of his. Something about a child. She [Colette?] went on to Ravel about his daughter and Ravel replied with icy formality *But I have no daughter.*

No daughter, Alan thought. No daughter. The piano notes shimmered and fell like an avalanche in the sun. Chords of rapture and regret. The earrings winked and sparkled next to Jessica's face.

Alan walked down the path towards town. He felt an open road jocund feeling of hope. He passed the graveyard. Someone had vandalized a stone cross. Next to the broken cross was a small stone lamb. A child's grave. There were other stone lambs. Perhaps a turn of the century epidemic. He felt a pang and paused on the sundappled path. Some local stone mason had done a brisk business with that lamb model. All the sickness that took children in those days. Infant mortality.

All the sunshine didn't help. Sun on dancing leaves. Someone on the path behind him was singing "Greensleeves" in a trained voice. He went on, quickening his pace. A shadow moved beside him like a small intent animal. He could hear the river, far off, incessantly falling. It sounded like an old man telling an interminable story while dozing off.

Alan's wife had left him in the autumn of 1988. She left him as one might leave a doctor's waiting room, with brisk preoccupation, thinking of where she was going next. She didn't blame him. It was just that he was suddenly irrelevant. Some men, Alan knew, coped with divorce by sitting in sweat lodges, hugging one another and chanting. He had avoided all that. He had survived the divorce on his own. But the other thing—

The summer of 1988 had been uneasy. There were record heat waves all over the country. There was drought and scanty crops. Miles of beaches on the East Coast had been closed after hazardous medical wastes washed up. Children had played with hypodermic needles. Fierce fires in the forests of the Pacific Northwest had been fought by armies of firefighters. The AIDS quilt grew. There was talk about the ozone layer or the lack of it. Black corrosive stuff bubbled up through cracks in a playground adjacent to an elementary school near Chicago. There had been skin disorders in the school's population.

Alan's daughter had not gone to this school. Her school was safely a mile away. That summer she drowned in the public swimming pool in plain sight of crowds of people. Two alert trained lifeguards had done everything they knew, all that they could.

The mountains from this distance looked like somnolent furry beasts. There were folds in their fur. Muscles were slack or bunched up under the fur. All around Alan was vigorous opulent nature—stern saguaro, the mountains and the far-off muttering river.

Yet even in this stunning sunlight Alan knew pernicious human evil lurked. He had heard stories of communes out in the desert. Survivalists, satanists, cultists of all kinds. Stories of people who disappeared while camping or just traveling through. Bodies were sometimes found. Children died—

He walked on down and went into the roadhouse. A big neon sign hung over the doorway: Q.T. The sign was, of course, not on. Inside was a big barny room with tables circled around a dancefloor. There was a bandstand. Two men in bib overalls sat at one end of the bar. He sat about halfway down and ordered a beer. A big sign over the cash register said *Quittin Time*. That explained the place's name.

"Quiet today" he said.

The bartender, a young man who looked as if he worked out

seriously, nodded slowly.

"Come back this weekend," said the bartender. "A whole different scene then."

"I just might do that," Alan said.

One morning Alan found a note that had been slipped under his door. *Why have you erected this wall between us? We must talk—*

The note was signed "J." Which one? What did it mean? All three were cordial with him but nothing more. Perhaps the note had been put under the wrong door. But it was Caspar on one side and two of the young bunheads on the other.

When he saw the three "J's" later, together or alone, everything seemed normal. Was it a joke? A put-on? He waited for some sign, a look, a word, another note.

The following weekend he went down to the Q.T. As he came in a woman was on the bandstand singing "You ain't woman enough to take my man." She wore skintight jeans and boots and a t-shirt with someone's face on it. From his distance Alan thought it looked like Franz Kafka but that didn't seem to make sense. The woman had a thin hardscrabble face like someone in a Dorthea Lange photograph. Alan thought she looked like a lesbian, but the way she was belting out the song seemed to belie that notion.

Alan sat at the bar. The tables were crowded with men wearing ten gallon hats and women in a variety of outfits. Some wore granny dresses, some were dressed like the woman who was singing and some wore buckskin skirts. One man had a sweeping piratical plume on his hat. His belt was hung with silver conchos which were the size of salad plates. Each concho must have weighed ten pounds. He was not a big man.

When the singer finished, there was enthusiastic applause. The band announced a new song: *Honkey Tonk Heaven.* With the opening chords the dancefloor was full. There was a flourish of expertise, rhythmic bootstomping, square-dance style ducking under arms, promenading. Alan felt like a caliph in disguise.

He sipped his beer, looked around, absorbed the good feeling. There was a confident exuberant frontier air to the place, the music, the people, the dancing. He felt buoyed up. He stayed until closing. Then he went up the dark path towards the Colony humming *Your Cheatin Heart.*

The next weekend he went back. The band was playing something slow. Couples hugged and swayed. He went to the washroom. On his way down the dark hallway someone brushed past him going the other way. Jeanne? The corridor was dark and narrow. He wasn't sure. There was dubious paper on the walls, stained, ripped, hanging. When he came out of the washroom the person who had passed him was deep in conversation with someone at the other end of the corridor. The couple looked, somehow, lewd, sinister. He couldn't tell if it were Jeanne or not.

The band was still playing the slow set. *Please don't tell me how the story ends*—And there, over there it might have been Jeanne dancing with someone dressed in black. And there, was it Jessica dancing too close with a man in a black t-shirt? The man had a tattoo. And there was Jackie at a table leaning across to kiss someone who looked like a biker. He wasn't sure. The uncertain light—

The band announced the final song, *Blue Eyes Cryin in the Rain* and everybody was out on the dancefloor. Alan peeled at the label of his bottle. Then the lights went up. There was cheering and yip-yipping. He stood out in front while cars and pickup trucks revved and roared out of the gravel parking lot. The three girls did not come out. The neon sign went off. He started up the street and turned up the path back to the Colony. He was alone on the path. If it had been the girls they must have other plans. He had drunk a lot of beer. Halfway up he stopped to relieve himself. With the sound of urine splashing on the gravel came another sound, far-off. A cry, a howl. Perhaps a coyote.

There was a confusion of bird's singing. Alan woke up too suddenly. He was cramped onto the couch in his studio, curled up, neck hurting. He got up and moved awkwardly around the studio. He had worked late and lay down for what he planned to be only a rest.

It was very early in the morning. They weren't serving breakfast yet. He plugged in the kettle and made a cup of instant coffee. Sunlight on the studio windows hurt his eyes. It looked like a promising day. He sipped the coffee, and looked over last night's work.

The meeting of two saints—an abbot and an abbess—who converse. As they are deep in their dialogue, astonished watchers saw that they were elevated several feet above the convent floor, continuing to talk, ecstatic and high in the air—

It was confused. He would have to sort it out later, after it cooled off. He put the new pages on top of the almost finished draft and went off to breakfast. As he was locking the studio door he was conscious of someone standing behind him. He turned. It was Jeanne. She looked all washed out, eyes smudged, lips looked puffed.

"Alan?" she said. "Could I talk to you?"

They walked down the path. Jeanne began to tell him about her real life.

"Not my r-e-e-l life," she said with a crook of a laugh. "The thing of it is that I married this guy—he was a slug—well, I was young. Young-young. And I wanted to get away from home—from my father—He's such a fascist. But you know all about that—"

Alan wondered who, what he was supposed to know. Why was she telling him all this—

"Anyway the thing—the marriage—lasted about thirty minutes—took a year to finish off legally I mean. But I kept his name. I didn't want to go back to my father's name. I always thought it sounded stagey anyhow, you know?"

Jessica was coming down the path towards them. She seemed in a hurry. She smiled a quick hello at Alan and said something in a low voice to Jeanne. The two set off back towards the studios, smiling goodbye at Alan. Both were wearing shorts and hiking boots. Jessica had better legs than Jeanne.

"Thanks for listening," Jeanne called back to him.

There were no more notes under his door. His frieze of young women continued to be open and friendly. The note must have been meant for someone else. And the apparitions at the Q.T. must have been exactly that—projections of his own over-heated imagination, phantasms caused by too much beer drunk to loud music in a dark room.

The Monday of Alan's last week in residence, Jeanne turned up missing. She was supposed to go hiking with other people from the video program the previous Saturday. When she didn't show, they went on without her. But when she didn't make it to a Monday morning critique session they got worried. Security staff searched her room. Her wallet was in the dresser. It looked as if all her clothes and toiletries were there.

State police from Santa Fe came up. Alan saw Jessica and Jackie in troubled conversation in a lounge. He wondered if he should tell the police about the Q.T. About the dangerous look-ing man. Maybe Jackie and Jessica knew something—

Maybe she was off on some innocent lark with someone innocent, someone from the Colony. But the wallet. Blasco walked around the place in a distraught daze. Jeanne was his daughter. Nobody had ever mentioned that to Alan. Everybody seemed to know it and probably assumed that he did too.

He walked out in the parking lot behind the residence and across towards the studios. Abstract oil stains were etched into the parking lot concrete. Like splashes of blood. Bushes at the border of the lot had sudden yellow blossoms on them. He looked up at the bland morning sky. A girl asleep in a meadow, tousled hair tangled in the grass and timothy. Oh child of the pure unclouded brow—

Alan wondered if his reading should be cancelled. Good taste and all—

"No, no," said Alison, the resident counselor. "You must do the reading. The Colony's business must go on—"

She went on in her calm counselor's voice. Alan did his reading.

"This piece," he began "is called *The Marriage of Heaven and Hell*. Besides the obvious Blake thing I wanted to work in nuances inspired by a piece by Ravel—*L'Enfant et les sortilages*. I must have listened to it a hundred times while I was working. I toyed with the idea of playing a tape as background music for this reading—"

Polite laughter. He began: "Two rabbis discussed and disputed as they walked—"

Caspar came up to the podium as the crowd was breaking up.

"Alan," Caspar said slowly. "What you have achieved—my young friend—Extraordinary. The pain—so formal, restrained. What? Grief under pressure. Mystical. The rapture—the regret—"

"Caspar," Alan said, crouching down next to the podium, looking into Caspar's face. "I don't know what I did. I don't understand it."

Caspar shook his head slowly.

"But you don't need to," said Caspar. "It is not given to you. To understand. Yes?"

Blasco was standing out in the parking lot next to piles of luggage. He looked as if he did not know where he should be. He looked like a large hollow statue. Alan went up to him, tried to say daughter, your daughter but could not. Blasco took his hand in both of his. Alan gripped Blasco's shoulder. It felt frail, breakable. Neither man spoke. Blasco looked deep into Alan's face as if he knew.

Alan sat in the back of the van. Jessica was in the seat ahead of him, wearing big sunglasses, looking subdued, pensive. No sign of Jackie. The van pulled out of the lot and onto the road. Alan looked back but he could not see Blasco. Maybe

Jeanne would show up, penitent, having been off someplace thoughtlessly. He thought of a dried-up river bed, fissured and cracked and a hurried grave dug in the river's bank. The van turned past the graveyard. There was the Halleck mausoleum. He could not see any of the small stone lambs.

The van turned on the road through town, passing the Q.T. which was silent and shutdown with its empty parking lot looking large. One of the van's tires struck a sewer manhole cover which clanged like a sullen iron bell.

On the highway leading south past Chimayo was a small church where pilgrims came to pray and touch the sacred earth. Many had come there and been healed. A small room was filled with canes, supports and crutches. They would not, of course, stop at the church. Alan tried to form words in his mind. A prayer for all children lost in the dark. Oh Lord, he thought, Oh Lord. The van went on past Chimayo towards Santa Fe.

FOX TROT

1.   a short broken slow trotting gait in which the hind foot of the horse hits the ground a trifle before the diagonally opposite forefoot.

2.   a ballroom dance in duple time that includes slow walking steps, quick running steps, and the step of the two-step.

Kate had let a car cut in on the access to the expressway and he didn't even wave or nod thanks, just took his cut as if it were divine right. The injustice smarted. And then, because she had slowed to allow the cut, some jerk behind her was laying on the horn and then hurtled past, giving her the finger without looking, his horn dopplering. Her eyes smarted with tears. If only there would be a cop up ahead and she'd pass the jerk sitting head down in his car, the roof lights on the cruiser flashing and circling.

But she knew no justice lay ahead of her down the road. She had just dropped her husband off at the airport. As usual he had insisted she not come in.

"At our age," he had said, "Fervent goodbyes are unseemly, aren't they?"

She had agreed although she did not. Agree. She had left him at the curb outside the terminal. In the rearview mirror it looked as if some woman were walking towards him or they were walking towards one another and not quite in the direction of the terminal's automatic doors. Towards one another. As if they were not strangers.

Peter went to London for three or four days on business each month. Once Kate came with him and they tacked a vacation on to the business. That happened only once. He claimed that he did not enjoy these trips. The only extracurricular activity he indulged in was the occasional bespoke suit.

Kate feared that something was going on. He was pushing thirty-nine. This was going to be a crucial time. All the magazines said so. At home he was distant, preoccupied, made and received mysterious phone calls he said were about business. Sometimes she answered and got hang-ups. Confrontation, she had read was not a good tactic. Tenacious silence until the fever died down was better. Kate had her doubts about either tactic.

For many years Peter had endured those "Does your nose come with your glasses?" jokes. Just a few years ago he tried contacts and suddenly women were all over him. It wasn't just the glasses, Kate thought. Some men age better than others. Peter looked like an older, more distinguished Clark Kent. Without the glasses.

Kate and Peter had met in the first year of university. Peter was heading for med school and she wanted to be a teacher like her father. Their instant romance, tempestuous, rocky, hot, troubled, stretched all the way to graduation. Peter had switched to Business (he could always silently blame Kate for abandoning the medical career, but let's be fair, he did bubkes in biology) Kate majored in English but did not go on for an MA nor did she go to teacher's college. She was pregnant.

They were married the summer after graduation and Peter went with Kuhn Associates. Sounds like a German consortium but was Japanese. They made things like seat belts for the automotive industry.

So they moved to Windsor, where Candy was born. Peter and Kuhn were good for one another. Kuhn went from being fifteen in the field the year they hired Peter to second place the year Candy went off to drama school in Montreal.

When Kate got home, there was a message from her mother on the answering machine. From Barcelona. Said she'd call later. Which didn't help Kate. Which clock was her mother on? Kate pictured her mother at a sidewalk cafe table, superb legs crossed, a dainty opened sandal dangling from one slim foot. She gave great sandal-dangle.

Later on, Kate put a Vaughan-Williams CD on. *The Lark in the Clear Air.* It made her think of the downs in Sussex where she had seen lambs on the hills on that one-time trip. She wondered what Peter was doing right now in London where there were no lambs.

She went to bed. For a long time she tossed around, kept looking at the alarm. The green digital numbers moved on, implacable. Finally she fell asleep and dreamed of storms in the mountains where she and her mother were stranded at a foreign airport. She woke up feeling dread. She must have gone back to sleep because the phone yanked her awake.

"Hello? Kate? Kate?"

"Daddy?" she said, looking at the alarm. Four AM. "What's wrong?"

"It's your mother," came the voice, tired and petulant. "She's left me."

"No, Daddy, she's at this *conference*—"

"The conference is over," came the tired voice. "She phoned to tell me that she was going on to some place in Greece. I think she's with that twit, whatsisname. Kate, I don't know what to *do*."

Kate made soothing noises, tried for the rational approach, knew that tenacious silence wouldn't work in this case, what the hell could she do about it anyway. She was thousands of miles from Arizona and from Greece or Spain or wherever Sally was right now, four-fifteen AM in Windsor.

Finally she got her father quieted down enough to hang up and she promised to call him later (for what? for what?) She sat on the edge of the bed staring down at the floor. She loved her father. She loved both of her parents. But she had always wondered how two such radically different people had gotten together. Herbert and Sally. Now, Sally was twelve years younger than Herbert. But that wasn't the real problem.

Herbert had never *been* Herbert. He had never been Herb or Herbie. He was H.J. Sally might have cried out *O Herbert!* in the throes of youthful lovemaking, but in public Herbert had escaped his name. Someone once remarked to him that poor Emerson had been burdened with two of the dumbest names in the language: Ralph and Waldo. H.J. laughed in agreement but in petto felt that his own name ranked high on the dumb list.

H.J. was something of a stick. He was seventy and had been retired for five years. But he had been preparing for retirement ten years before the event. He investigated savings plans and tax shelters and went to seminars and sent for brochures about property in Costa Rica, Texas, Mexico, the Cayman Islands and Florida. The summer vacations in that preparatory decade had been spent in visits to potential golden age residences: condos in South Carolina, villas in Georgia. Places like that. For ten years Sally had put up with it. Being dragged (as she put it to Neil. More on him later) from one geriatric staging place on the railroad to death so long before the fact.

Before the golden age hunt, the summers had been spent on Civil War battlefields where they walked where Grant or Jackson had. H.J. was a history professor. Never, back then, she said to Neil, had she uttered a word of complaint. About how she wanted the Costa Brava or the South of France. In Gettysburg she said the names, whispered to the night motel ceiling, her lips pursed as if to kiss: *the South of France.* It might have been on the banks of Antietam Creek that she decided to seek a Life of Her Own.

Later on, Sally might say in conversation "Where I'm from right now is Arizona." This should have alerted H.J. It signalled a sense of the transitory, of muted distaste for that place. For Sally, echoing G. Stein, there was no *there* there. The retirement condo was for Sally, like the motel rooms in Vicksburg or Richmond or the golden age villas in Georgia, a place to pass through on the way to the real place.

H.J. didn't pick up the signals. Not only because he was a stick, but because he was a decent person who felt in his comfortable way that he had a decent wife, a decent marriage, a decent child, had his decent career and now had a right to his decent retirement.

Sally didn't think decent cut it. Maybe her leaving H.J. might be judged as akin to someone running from a burning and doomed building. Who wanted to be burned decently to death?

Maybe there would have been trouble even without all of H.J.'s quirks. Sally had always been trouble. She had blue eyes which in certain lights looked grey. There was a small complex of laugh wrinkles around her eyes. Her hair was worn longer than was fashionable for mature women. It was thick and dark and streaked and tipped with grey. If it were blonde it would have been called a *tawny mane.*

Trouble. Look: Sally didn't just get *in* or *out* of a car. She choreographed the action. Getting out: The car pulls smoothly into the driveway. The engine is cut. She takes her prescription sunglasses off, bends her head to put them in her purse, opens the door, car keys dangling from her hand (the bunch of metal held thus delicately draws attention to the fragility of the hand) and she rises from the seat, from the car, emerges like a sea nymph ascending from foam to walk toward wherever she was going.

Getting in: An artful reversal of the getting out: swinging legs in so there is a blur of floating garment. Head bent to the purse to extract the glasses and the keys after the door thuds shut. The thunk of the door and the bent head peering into the purse. Polarities of heavy technology and softly feminine. The bent head effects a curve of the neck which, when coupled with the somewhat distracted peering into the purse, gives an edge of the sweetly vulnerable. Bent neck is just the right touch of delight in disorder.

When she walked. O boy. When she walked from or to a car or wherever, her skirt swayed and hovered in countrapuntal motion over her legs. The simple innocent motor action drew attention, accidentally? absent-mindedly? to the essential mystery of female skirts: What they conceal as they hover, bell-like over. *Under.* Sally was trouble.

Sally was trouble at any age. What she did to her history professor Herbert (H.J.) Boothe when she was twenty and took his popular Civil War course. She sat in the front row, gave him knee, thigh, the hair hanging over the notebook, the pencil propped against pursed lips. They were married right after stacked arms at Appomattox and final exams. Now, thirty-eight years later, Sally was pushing fifty-eight, looked sort of forty if one thought about it and had presumably dumped her husband.

Listen. *She* had tried. She looked up Southwestern decor in *Architectural Digest*. She just did not cotton to adobe and tile and big clay pots. She suggested Santa Fe but H.J. said they had mean winters. Who wanted winters in the golden years?

After Kate grew up and left home Sally got restless. Although she looked the type she did not want to play tennis or golf. She did volunteer work at the art gallery, made contacts, got a part-time job at a private gallery and went on the board of the local arts council. The following year she was elected Chair of the board and then this government job posting came.

There was H.J., five years from retirement and his wife was suddenly getting on and off airplanes going all over the country and the world. For the Arts.

So she had seduced her professor. So what. She had been a good Fifties wife, except that she never did a casserole. She bore a child, was a good mother, they had fine if not operatic sex, she was supportive—look at all those battlefields explored with a nary a tisk of complaint.

For years H.J. had suffered from a sense of injured merit. His list of achievements was sparse: an article published or paper delivered once a year, a book on the Peninsular Campaigns bravely begun, fussed with, over-researched and never finished. His reputation as a popular teacher turned into a reputation among his colleagues as shallow flashiness and among the students as the equivalent of an easy lay. H.J. thought he deserved more recognition. He *knew* he was something of a stick. But he was hardworking, diligent, anxious, faithful. Above all, decent. A decent stick.

And there was Kate, caught between her parents, emotionally and geographically. She loves her father but pities him. She loves her mother but from a wary distance. She sees Sally as a kind of life force, or at least a force in *her* life. Kate had always felt she was in her mother's shadow.

Her mother came on as if in technicolor. Kate felt like a black and white rerun. Kate relished the ordinary. People in Kate and Peter's circle were always putting Windsor down as a place to live. She kept her silence. She liked living in Windsor. In a similar way she secretly liked the food served on airplanes. It was fashionable to bum-rap Windsor and airplane food but she wasn't in fashion. The neatness, the cold silverware wrapped in the napkin, the precise positions of the entree portions, the piece of cheese neat in its cellophane. All those things to be unwrapped severally. There was about it a sense of order and piety, like the canonical hours, a rite that took up some of the travel time.

Peter liked to complain about airplane food. He was also one of those who denigrated Windsor.

Sally phoned from Athens to tell Kate that she was going to this small island for a week or so.

"Mom," Kate said. "Daddy phoned. He's very upset."

There was a transatlantic sigh.

"Katie, I don't know what to *do*," Sally said. "I just cannot go back to that upright tomb they call a condo. There are people there with actual *blue* hair. I *mean* it. I am not ready to die. I don't want to hurt your father...Well, we'll have to see when I get back—"

No mention of whatsisname. With all the brouhaha with her parents, Kate had pushed her own problem to the back of her mind. It didn't go away.

She decided to take a walk. Not that it would solve anything. It just seemed like a healthy, sensible thing to do. In Windsor, everything tends towards the river. That was where she went.

The view across the river was blurred. Kate took her smudged glasses off, breathed on them and cleansed them. That was better. A girl in a dark coat passed her swiftly, long hair loose, intent on where she was hurrying to. Another young woman stood leaning on the iron fence a few yards ahead of her. The young woman was shielding her eyes against the setting sun. The hand dropped to cover one eye and became a gesture of regret. A ship passed, heading down river towards Lake Erie. Through her cleansed glasses Kate could see the number markings, the—what— Plimsoll? numbers that said the ship was riding high with an empty hold.

Three young girls passed her going in the opposite direction. Each had a tattoo on a bare shoulder. It was too chilly to be out without a coat. One tattoo was a spider, one was a flower, possibly a rose, and the third seemed to be a bat in flight.

On the balcony for each unit there were two wicker chairs and a small table that one might write a postcard at or set out a bowl of fruit or cut flowers on. Flowers in clay pots were set out there. One of these was a small, green-leaved tree in a Southwestern style pot. H.J. had found out that this was a ficus. Something pink bloomed in a Roman villa style vase.

He woke to the sound of falling water and saw through the sliding doors the ficus shaken by rain. In this season, in this area, rain was sparse. He thought of General Grant under a tree out of the rain at Shiloh. He stuck it out. He won. He could just as easily have lost. Once Grant said "Tethered as we are by the iron chain of circumstance something something—" The phrase was soothing, and he went back to sleep.

He was walking in mist, trees hung down low along the path, low before him, heavy with rainwater. In the dim light each bead of rain on the branches glimmers. If he were to touch them they would scatter and fall. A small brook has broken through and the path is full of water. Mist on the mountain top was caught up there like cloth on a barb. Trees like needles prodded the sky. Now the clouds were tearing loose from the crest and floated off, hung indifferently.

Then he was on a dark ship moving through a night sea. The sharp bow furrowed the water. Then he was on placid concrete steps which were gently crumbling. Where was the ship? The sun had fully set but a lingering light was on the stone figures he walked toward, those stone figures with folded arms. He was in a backyard that looked like his mother's. There were two empty lawn chairs at the far end of the yard. A tree's leaves suddenly came alive in a spurt of wind, like a rush of young dancers. And there, coming towards him, was his granddaughter, a child again, smiling. He heard a joyous chorus of horns and a distant choir of children's voices, too far off to make out the words. *Home* he thought they sang and *rivers and mountains far from home.*

He awoke, clutching his throat. The dream must have something to do with Sally leaving, but oddly enough he felt this morning more alert, more alive than he had for a long time. He decided to get dressed in his Mall walking clothes and have breakfast there.

All over the world airplanes are taking off, ascending, descending, landing. Travelers arrive at Departure lounges, relatives gather at Arrivals. A plane over the Atlantic rises to meet the rising sun. A plane heading for California chases the sun. Ships leave the harbor or come into home port. Everywhere, people are on the move. Retirees in RVs gather at rest stops in the Southwest to exchange stories of where they are from and where they are going.

As she turned onto her street, the sun had fully sunk and suffused afterglow lit up the sky over the river. The street lights weren't on yet. For some antic reason a jaunty jingle bounced in her memory:

In Heaven there'll be no algebra
No learning dates and names
But only playing golden harps
And reading Henry James.

Kate smiled. She had been singular in the Modern Novel course for liking James. The rest of the class moaned and complained all through *The Ambassadors*. She and the teacher—Dr. Hamilton—had been alone in relishing the fine, delicate nuances.

Back in the house, she looked for the book. There it was, stuck between Updike's *Couples* and *The Book of Daniel*. There was her name on the inside cover. Kate Boothe. Her real, original name. The Norton Critical Edition. There were the underlined passages and margin comments in her handwriting. The twenty year old girl who underlined these sentences and made the comments in the margin, who wrote the word *irony* there. Serious, oh so serious and so young. Now she felt like a distant relative of that girl as she read her comments.

She turned to the scene in Gloriani's garden where Strether suddenly realizes at the age of fifty-five that his life is almost over and he hasn't really lived yet. *Live all you can* he says to a young friend.

James's house was down in Rye, in Sussex. They hadn't gotten there. She had wanted to. Why hadn't they?

She could go to graduate school. Why not? She could get her MA. There was no reason why not. Live all you can. She could do her thesis on James. There had to be *someone* in the department who shared her enthusiasm for James. She turned back to the first chapter and began to read again. If only it were morning so she could call the university, get the thing started. She wanted to get started.

He drove to the Mall. Lots of retirees spent their day there. It was air-conditioned and pleasant. It was what the old village square must have been like. The sun was intense, personal. Clouds, aloof, indifferent, grand, tall as horses stepping, moved across the mountain ridge in the distance. On a clump of rocks in a landscaped area two small animals (Squirrels? but a different color than he knew—) scrambled around like hands on a map, trying to find out where they were or where to go.

In the Mall, a girl who looked like Kate had in her twenties was walking towards him, talking excitely to her friend. She had the same big eyes, the expressive eager face, the same bird-flight hand gestures. Walked the same way too, a kind of dancing, with a trace of a child's impetuosity in it. He felt ashamed of having called her, laid his burden on her.

The friend listening with her thin alive face, wide lips smiling as she listened, listening with grace—that was what he missed most about teaching—the constant presence of the young with all their hope and verve. There was also, of course, the selfishness and blatant egotism. He did not miss some things. After they had passed, he glanced back at their blue-jeaned buns. When, oh when would he be free of the sexual itch that must be scratched? Since he had been, what, twelve or so— meant almost sixty years of obsessive craziness, compulsive wanking, posing, hankering, showing off, peeking, peering, panting, timewasting, furtiveness and, oh yes, *noticing*. So much wetness and heavy breathing. One wants to think there are other things in life, more important. Oh? says his aged groin, and just what are they?

He got a danish and coffee and sat at a table under the sky-light. "Excuse me," said a man at the next table. He and his wife were wearing matching T-shirts that said *I Survived San Francisco*.

"I see by your shirt that you're a native," said the man.

H.J. was wearing a blue shirt with *Arizona* on it in red letters.

"Not really," said H.J. "Only been here about five years. They don't consider you a native until you've been here a lot longer—"

"That's the way it is most places," said the man's wife.

She had very white hair and very blue eyes.

"Well," said the man. "We're shopping around for a place to retire. So far this looks really good."

"I like it," said H.J. "My wife would have preferred New Mexico. But they have winters there. I've had enough winters."

"So have we," laughed the woman. "We're from Minneapolis."

"I'm from Ontario," said H.J. "I can't stay here year round. I have to keep up my medical plan."

The man and woman looked serious and interested. Americans got all wet over the Canadian medical plan.

"I guess I'm what they call a snowbird," H.J. laughed.

"Say," said the man. "Why don't you join us? Our name is Godden. Henry and Lola Godden."

"Thanks," said H.J. "I'm Herbert. Herbert Boothe. I used to teach history."

"Say, that was some rain last night," said Henry.

"It's about all we'll get for a month," said Herbert.

Older people, mostly couples, some in matching outfits of some light synthetic material, were walking purposefully. Taking the air, one might say, or more precisely, taking the indoor conditioned air. Younger people in groups walked more slowly, eating ice cream cones, laughing immoderately at private jokes. Intent shoppers carrying treasures in plastic bags passed patient seated men waiting for their wives. Herbert saw it frozen for a moment, like a tableau depicting life in all its burgeoning disorder. Only death was neat, shapely with its beguiling comfort of clean stillness. The moment passed and everyone moved to a singular rhythm.

"I can give you the name of my condo managers," Herbert smiled at his new friends. The air above the skylight seemed rinsed and fresh.

Kate was reading "The Beast in the Jungle." It was about a man who waited all his life for some big thing to happen. The big thing, he found out in horror, was that nothing would happen. He would be a man who had not lived at all. Like Strether in *The Ambassadors*. Seemed to be a theme of some concern to James. Well, Kate thought, it *was* a Big Theme. If you haven't had your life, what have you had?

Neil was in the boat's small lounge moaning and retching. A penchant to seasickness, Sally thought, was not in itself a symptom of character weakness. But Neil was playing the *young man* bit rather hard. Let's face it, she thought, he's supposed to be this *young* documentary film maker and he spends more time at conferences and on panels than behind the camera.

She stood at the rail near the bow. Although the sea was rough, the sky was clear and the water was the deepest blue she had ever seen. She remembered an ink from grade school called *Quink*. That was the color: quink blue. A man she presumed was the captain kept walking past her, smiling helpfully. Ogod the Shirley Valentine thing. Here she was thousands of miles from home—wherever that was—on her way to whatever it was, idyl, dirty vacation with someone for whom whatever original attraction she had felt was ebbing away astern as fast as the boat's progress. She wondered if they had nunneries in Greece.

"But I wanted to go to Albert Hall. Yo Yo Ma is there."

"I know. I couldn't get tickets, remember?" he said.

"He won a Grammy last year. I was so looking forward to it," she pouted prettily.

This used to work.

"The Grammy was the year before," Peter said.

In a little while Peter said he had an appointment with his tailor. He went out and walked in the direction of Albert Hall where he could have gotten tickets for tonight. There were all these little foreign embassies in the area. Many Arab emirates. Lots of alert looking people around that were obviously security.

He didn't have an appointment with his tailor. He just wanted to get away, out, by himself. For the first time in months he found himself wishing the trip were over, that he was headed back to Windsor. It was, after all, home, and Kate was there.

He walked towards the Victoria and Albert Museum. There was a pub near here, behind Albert Hall, where the musicians went after a performance. A wonderful little place. He had been there once, but was never able to find the place afterwards. He decided to try again.

There was a constant process of renovating going on in the area, workmen's vans all over and piles of lumber crowding the walkways.

Now he was in what seemed to be an alleyway, with garage doors all the way to the corner. It looked unpromising.

And then there it was, around the corner. In the mild weather, some of the patrons had taken their drinks outside, and stood, casually talking. The interior was dim and quiet. He ordered a half pint of bitter.

"On holiday?" said a man with a full head of thick curly hair standing next to him.

"Business," said Peter. "I'm heading home tomorrow."

"Well, safe journey," said the man, raising his glass.

"Thanks," said Peter. "I like it here, but home's home."

In one of Henry James's non-fiction works he recounts a recurring dream, or nightmare he had as a boy: He was in one of the galleries of the Louvre alone at night. Someone began to pursue him down the corridors. He ran, opening and closing doors with the unseen pursuer right behind him.

Then at one closed door, as he turned the knob he was aware that someone was tentatively turning the knob from the other side. Then the unseen person on the other side of the door tried to keep him from opening it. It was his pursuer. Now James knew, in the dream, that the roles were reversed. The quarry became the hunter. The hunter became the prey. The dream chase went on.

A man with blue innocent eyes and a white spade-shaped beard is wearing a shapeless wide-brimmed hat. He looks like the composer Charles Ives. He is wearing a blue T-shirt under a denim jacket. The blue T-shirt has the word *Arizona* on it in red. It is Herbert. He is about to board a bus that will take him to a staging area for a White Water rafting trip. Last night he phoned his daughter to tell her where he was going and to say he was sorry for having burdened her with trouble she could do nothing about.

He'd had a range of options for this adventure—from the Evening Float Trip to the Ultimate! White Water. He chose the Daily White Water which was somewhere in between. He feels at this moment essentially light and free.

From her window Sally could see the road winding down to the sea. There was a taverna and a dock down there. If she looked out the window to the right, she could see the road going on between the stone walls and up a hill.

The road and the stone walls reminded her of a picture in a child's book—perhaps Kate's, maybe her own—a road going past a stone wall and cows in a field looking over the wall. There is a stile in the wall. And there is a crooked man with a crooked stick. His face cannot be seen in the picture. Only his bent back, his hand leaning on the knobbed stick as he makes his painful way up the road that curves up the hill to a point where the road becomes a dot. Behind that dot was nothing. Here, there were no cows and no crooked man but the road rose to vanish in a dot at the top of the hill where it met the sky. Behind that dot was nothing. She looked sharply ahead at the dock and the taverna and the boats rocking in the morning waves. The scene was comforting.

Peter was on his plane, homeward bound. He was thinking of an *L.A. Law* rerun he had seen recently. Arnie was caught in flagrante. His new wife found out. He was penitent. She was obdurate. Despite the fact that her little girl loves Arnie (So does the wife—) she can't respect him anymore. Thus a quickie leads to blooie. No eraser on that pencil.

Peter felt a sullen disquiet. What chances he had taken with his precious life, as if he had all the time in the world. Maybe things would be all right. Maybe he hadn't mucked things up irreparably. He almost began to pray.

All over the world, airplanes are taking off, ascending, descending, landing. Travelers arrive at Departure lounges, relatives gather at Arrivals. White boats ride at anchor in blue water. Rivers run white and green and clear over black rocks. People are stirring and moving. It is a kind of small figure for human existence. We live, we die. And in that transience is our glory. We tell our fellow passengers stories to keep us awake and keep the darkness back. Stories of where we have been and where we are going.